Forward Ever!
Backward Never!

Michael Cozier

iUniverse, Inc.
New York   Bloomington

Forward Ever! Backward Never!

The views expressed in this work are solely those of the author and do not necessarily reflect the views of the publisher, and the publisher hereby disclaims any responsibility for them.

iUniverse books may be ordered through booksellers or by contacting:

iUniverse
1663 Liberty Drive
Bloomington, IN 47403
www.iuniverse.com
1-800-Authors (1-800-288-4677)

Because of the dynamic nature of the Internet, any Web addresses or links contained in this book may have changed since publication and may no longer be valid.

ISBN: 978-1-4401-5121-7 (sc)
ISBN: 978-1-4401-5122-4 (ebk)

Printed in the United States of America

iUniverse rev. date: 6/26/2009

Michael Cozier was born in Trinidad and Tobago and lives in Icacos Village with his wife, Anne, and two children, John and Hannah. *Forward Ever! Backward Never!* is his first book and it was marinated to perfection over two, long decades.

A foreword by the Editor

When I close my eyes, I can see it still: the bawdy boys' room in Icacos, the green fishnets heaped in one corner, the twenty watt bulb dangling precariously from a rafter, the smell of the sea and the roll of her waves in the distance, the watery eyes of squiffed sailors, the archaic double-decker which still survives, the incessant zing of mosquitoes which provoked curses and sudden slaps, the din of boys with wicked streaks, and the red *Panther* sitting on the top bunk, his legs dangling like airborne tassels, thrumming an iridescent, two-stringed toy guitar and singing extemporaneous ballads which spared none, an enormous, purple ledger, which we all knew as *the book with Uncle Michael's stories*, always at his side.

Today, almost twenty years later, that ledger, that vade-mecum, with all its scratches, complicated annotations and unfinished stories, has finally taken a form which can be easily shared with the world. In this book you will read concise works of fiction depicting *camaraderie*, lust, survival, hope, and perseverance which, somehow or the other, cleverly maintains a brilliant and wicked edge of humour in true *Trini* flavour and simultaneously delivers on the past, present and perhaps future façade of Icacos.

Michael Cozier *is* a master storyteller and *Forward Ever! Backward Never!* confirms that he *was* always a gem, hidden in plain sight on the boot tip of Trinidad and Tobago.

Lyndon Baptiste
Author of Boy Days

Contents

Frankie

I just one of them normal eighteen year old Icacos fellars out of school and loafing around. I just breezing out the days, when I need a lil money I go out to sea with the fisherman them or I ask the Old Man or the Old Lady and they fix me up nice, nice. I have a lil girlfriend right in the village name Emelia, well, to tell the truth, she not that good looking you know, but she have nice ways and the Old Lady and Old Man like she too bad. I know secretly they want me to marry Emelia and settle right there with them, me being their only child and all. Well, things was moving along real nice and then one day, just so, things take a drastic change. I come from playing football on the beach and start to take a bath from a barrel of rain water in the yard when I hear somebody say:

'Hello handsome.'

I look up and see a fine-looking girl in the neighbour's gallery. I say:

'Me?'

'Yes you, handsome,' she cajoled.

I start to blush right dey because nobody ever call me handsome. I say hello and brisk, brisk, hustle that bath and run inside because I only have on my underpants. When I done dry my skin and put on my clothes, I gone over in the Old Lady room, because my room doh have ah mirror, and I look in the mirror and say:

'Hello handsome.'

Well right away I know something wrong because the thing that looking back at me ain't have nothing handsome 'bout it, and I did done know that a'ready because my nickname in the village is *Double Ugly*. So I come to the conclusion that the girl either blind or she have a fascination with Beauty and the Beast.

Well, I gone out on the road and stand up, and along comes the neighbour's daughter, Patsy, with the same girl. Boy I never see ah human being looking like that; the girl beautiful from head to toe. I accustom to them Icacos girl with jigger in they foot and they toes sticking out in all directions, but if you see this girl foot… smooth like glass, man, she toes neat, neat and side-by-side, like soldiers when they marching, and talk 'bout pretty *cutex* on them toes. I say to myself right away: Frankie, this is the type of people you have to *sociate* with, boy.

Patsy introduce me to her: it was her cousin, Cindy, from San Fernando come to spend two weeks holidays. They said they were taking a walk by the shop and would see me later. When they were walking away the girl look back and say:

'Bye, handsome.'

I stand up there blushing like Mr. Masden's jackass and she look back at me and smiling. Now I hear people talking 'bout love at first sight and ah hear some folks using some big word like *infracturation* or someting like that. Right now I feel like I somewhere between the two… because I stand up there feeling weak, weak and like my heart melting in me chest; I have to go home and sit down in the gallery *fust* ah feeling weak.

Seven o'clock that night, Patsy calling:

'Frankie! Frankie! Frankie!'

I watch outside.

'Me and Cindy going for ah walk on the beach, yuh want to come with we?'

Well I done outside and ready to go. I ain't tell the Old Lady and Old Man *nothing* and I gone touristin' on the beach with Cindy and Patsy. We walk for hours, Cindy asking me questions about fishing, Venezuela, the stars in the sky and every now and then she would touch me or bounce me gently. The next thing you know, she slip her hand into my left hand, well boy! I swear to God I get a stroke on my left side, only thing, if is so a stroke does feel I want to get one over my whole body, everyday of the year. I never feel so nice in my life. I have to pinch myself to make sure I not dreaming, me, *Double Ugly*, walking hand-in-hand with this beautiful girl on the Icacos beach. When I get home that night I can't sleep. I count sheep, goat, then fowl and start back counting sheep again, but I still can't sleep. I start walking up and down in the bedroom until my father say:

'Frankie, wat happen boy?'

I say, 'Old Boy, ah getting trouble to sleep.'

Well the Old Man come over in my room and sit down on the bed. Now me and the Old Man does live like brothers so when he ask me what happen I tell him the whole story, but I leave out the handsome part because I know he *go* laugh so hard he go wake up the whole village. The Old Man sit down there very thoughtful and when I finish he say:

'Frankie, this is a very serious thing, boy. Think of how Emelia will feel if she hear 'bout this. Emelia really love you, boy. Them *town girl* will only use you up and dump you like a hot potato. Now try to get some sleep.'

He pat me on the back and gone back in his room.

Well everything the Old Man tell me like it just pass through one ears and come out the next, because ah still can't sleep and I can't get the city girl out of my mind. I praying for morning to come so I could *fratanise* with her again.

The next day the girl come across by me early, wearing a short pants so tight and so short and so clinging that my hair raise. I was sitting on the step playing with Suzy and she come and sit down right beside me. She took away Suzy from me and placed her on her lap – Suzy was a pet cat my mother kept. My father come out in the gallery and say:

'Listen young lady, that is not the way to attire yourself when you coming around decent people.'

Well she just got up and went back over. I say:

'Old Boy, yuh didn't have to be so harsh with the girl, man, she only a stranger you know.'

'Listen Frankie! That girl will put you in trouble, boy,' he say.

Around lunch time, I take a stroll out by the shop and she and Patsy came to meet me. I say:

"I sorry 'bout the Old Man."

She say, 'No scene really,' and smiled.

Then Patsy told me how they open a new drive-in cinema in Point Fortin and they charging two dollars a car load and how she and Cindy want to go real bad but they don't have no money.

'Well that sounding like a good lime… but how we coming back?' I asked, since I know this drive-in thing is a night business.

'Well, we could hire a car to go and come back,' said Cindy.

Now I have a lil change save up and the plan sounding good, so I say:

'Don't worry 'bout the money. I'll take care of that.'

And I leave them and gone over by a fellar name Lakhan who own a taxi in the village, and ask him how much it go cost to hire him to go to the drive-in in Point Fortin. He said six dollars. I say:

'That sounds like a deal,' and gone back and give the girls the good news. I told them to get ready for six o'clock and Lakhan would pick them up.

Around five in the evening I bathe, put on some nice clothes, douse my shirt and pants in cologne three times, and take out all my money I had saving in a brown paper bag and put it in my pocket. When I come outside the Old Man say:

'What! Whey yuh going dress up sharp so, boy?'

'I making a lil turn, Old Boy,' I say.

'Be careful!' he growled.

I gone straight by Lakhan house and tell him to pick up the girls six o'clock and he will meet me by the shop after. Lakhan pick up the girls and meet me by the shop. Boy! When I see that city girl I nearly flip! She looking like ah movie star that walk straight off a cinema screen. We start heading up the road, Lakhan driving slowly and dodging potholes, and I sitting there, spellbound by Cindy's beauty. When we reach by the drive-in I give the gate man two dollars and he opened the gate and let we pass. They showing a movie called *Jail House Rock*, starring Elvis Presley, and we take one of the speakers and hook it up on the car door. Well, I gone in the back seat and sit down with the girls and Lakhan hail ah fellar by the canteen and gone over to lime with him. The movie going real nice and when intermission time come Cindy say she feeling to eat fry chicken. I pull out my money from my pocket like a big shot and buy chicken for Cindy, Patsy, meself and Lakhan and we sit down there eating and things going real good because the *ambeeyance* nice.

When the movie finish I gone back in the front seat with Lakhan and we making the journey back home. The two girls drop asleep in the back seat and Lakhan like he want to do the same. I study have to box him on the side of his head for he not to run off the road. When we reach down I pay Lakhan and drop off by the shop, and tell him to drop the girls home. About ten minutes after I went home and sneaked into the house quietly so as not to disturb the old people and lay on my bed and drop off to sleep.

The next morning I get up and take a walk on the beach side, when I coming back I bounce up the girls; Cindy was looking unhappy. I say:

'What happening?' but they not answering and then Patsy tell me Cindy have a problem. 'What problem?'

'She need thirty dollars,' Patsy say.

'Thirty dollars!' I nearly scream.

'You have to help me, Frankie! I need it by tomorrow afternoon,' pleaded Cindy.

Well I so stupid I ain't even ask the girl what she want the money for. I tell she:

'Okay. I will get the money for you from my parents,' and I gone straight home and brace the Old Lady.

Well, the Old Lady ain't ask me a question. She gone in she purse and come back with a ten dollar bill. 'This is all I could afford,' she say and hand me the bill.

I take it, fold it up nice and small, put it in my pocket and give the Old Lady a big kiss. Then I gone and brace the Old Man, I say:

'Old Boy, you think you could loan me a twenty?'

'Twenty! What for?' he asked.

Well, I look up, then I look down, but me and the Old Man so good I can't lie to him I say:

'I want it to give to Cindy.'

'Boy! You must be mad! You think I will take my hard earned money and give you to give that unmannerly city girl? Look, Frankie, I tell you stay away from that girl!'

Well the heat on me, so I run down to the beach and dive in the water and take a good swim. Then I sit down on the beach and start to tax my brain to see how I could come up with the other twenty. My mind fall on a fellar in the village name Talbot. Well, Talbot is a fellar who always have money no matter how hard things is, so there and then I make up my mind: I going home, change my clothes and I going over by Talbot and brace him for a loan.

While I changing my clothes, I realise I had bathe in the sea with the ten dollar note that the Old Lady had give me. When I search in my pocket I only finding half of the thing;

the rest melt away in the sea water. Well I start to cuss myself because now I know I still need thirty dollars. Same time the Old Lady calling me:

'Frankie! Come and eat before Suzy interfere with you food.'

I not hungry at all, so I take the food, put it on the back step and allow Suzy to eat it, then I went back in the bedroom, pick up the piece of ten dollar note that was on the bed and place it in my pocket.

Talbot was sitting on the step in front of his door. I say:

'Talbot, I need to have a word with you, boy.'

'Come in man Frankie, come in. Now what can I do for you?' he asked.

'I need a loan, boy.'

'How much?' asked Talbot.

'Thirty dollars,' I replied.

'What! That is a hefty sum!' he exclaimed. 'Anyway,' he said and start to whisper, 'you in luck. I have something going down tonight. If you want, instead of borrowing this money you could work with me tonight and I would pay you thirty dollars.'

Well I so happy I say yes right away and Talbot tell me to meet him behind the Catholic Church for seven o'clock that night. I ain't even bother to ask him what we going to do.

Half-past-six I eat my dinner and I tell the old people I stepping out for a while. As I leaving, the two girls saw me and they come out.

'You get the thing?' asked Cindy.

'No. But I working on it.'

I left them and cruise down by the shop.

When it was seven o'clock I gone behind the church and meet an *omenous* looking Talbot. He was dressed in a black pants and black jersey and had a bag slung over his shoulder. In one hand he had a shovel and in the other a fork. He shove the fork into my hand and ordered:

'Walk!'

We began to walk along the Icacos main road first and then we branched off unto a track in the coconut fields. We walked for about an hour and then we picked up another track in a wooded area. I asked Talbot:

'What we going to do, man?'

'We going to dig for treasure, Frankie… treasure, boy… treasure,' he said.

We walked for another half hour and then we climbed up a steep hill. When we were at the top, I look down and realise that we were right over the Fullerton village Cemetery. I get frightened right away. I start to stutter:

'Ta-ta-ta-ta-ta-talbot, I didn't know tha-tha-tha-tha-that this trea-trea-trea-trea-treasure was in a cemetery.'

Talbot whispered:

'Sit down, Frankie, and let me tell you what really going on. This ain't no treasure hunt! This is serious business! And you have to tell me now if you want to work for this thirty dollars or not.'

'Well… yes, I really want the thirty dollars.'

He say:

'Listen carefully. I in a business with a funeral agency fellar name Lazarus from Penal. How it does work is like this: when they going to bury a person in a casket Lazarus would send word for me in the morning, telling me what cemetery they burying the person in. They bury the man in the evening, in the night I go and I dig up the casket, throw the dead back in the hole, bury it nice, putting back all the wreaths and flowers in place so nobody could suspect anything, then I clean up the casket. This time so Lazarus making he way down here with the hearse, by midnight he collect the casket, pay me my money and both of we gone separate ways.'

I say:

'Talbot, this is not a good thing you doing, boy.'

'Listen man, you want this money or not?'

Right away my mind gone back to Cindy and when I study that sweet, little darling I throw away all my decent years of upbringing and say:

'Alright ah go help you dig.'

We look around the cemetery until we found a grave with fresh flowers on it. Talbot check the cross out and find a black piece of cloth tied to it. He untied the cloth and dangle it in front my face:

'This is it! This is the code Lazarus does leave behind!'

He *unsling* the bag from his shoulder and began moving the flowers and wreaths a safe distance from the grave.

'This is to redecorate,' he said.

He took out a bottle of rum from his bag, broke the seal, started to sprinkle drops all around the grave, and suddenly he start to do a kind of funny dance and chanting a kind of voodoo song.

'What the hell you doing, man?' I demanded.

'You don't go into grave just like that, boy, you have to tie the dead first,' he said.

Well my hair raise and I wondering what the hell I get myself into. He took the shovel and mark a cross on the grave and order me:

'Time to dig!'

Well we start to dig and making good progress too, because the dirt fresh but my conscience beating me so I say:

'Talbot, you think it right for we to dig up this poor man and take his casket?'

He stopped digging and say:

'Aye! Leh we get this straight. First of all, is only rich people could buy casket, so the man ain't poor! And second, dead people can't own property so technically the casket not his own.'

Well, it sounded like a good argument to me so I continued digging. When we were close to the casket, he said:

'Stop using the fork now before you puncture the treasure,' and he laughed.

We began taking turns with the shovel and shortly after we were scraping away dirt from the top of the casket with we hands. Talbot opened the casket and a vicious odor came out, not stink, but more like a type of fish freshness. I covered my nose. He said:

'Hold the handle at the other end and lift.' Then he said, 'Now… the both of we tilting together. One-two-three,' and we tilt and the dead man fall down *boop* in the hole.

My blood crawl.

It was quarter-past-eleven in the Cedros Police Station and Sergeant Doyle, who was in charge of proceedings, was briskly but meticulously making his rounds of the charge room. Corporal Baptiste was at the desk, writing hurriedly in the station's diary, and Constable Singh was quietly arranging some papers on a desk near the doorway. After exchanging greetings the Sergeant said:

'Gentlemen, there have been reports of caskets being stolen from various cemeteries around the country. The thing is, only today a fellow was buried in a casket in the Fullerton cemetery. Although I don't think we have these kind of mad people in our district,' he scoffed incredulously and continued, 'it might not be a bad idea for the both of you to take a drive down to the Fullerton Cemetery and have a look around.'

When we got the dead man out of the casket, Talbot climbed out of the hole, went into his bag and took out two pieces of rope. He passed the frizzled ends to me and instructed me to tie them to the two handles of the casket. After doing this, I climbed out of the hole and we held on to the ropes and pulled the casket to the surface. Talbot then took a piece of rag from the bag and a tin of polish and started to clean up the casket.

The lights from a vehicle was coming up the cemetery road and I pose off to run but Talbot consoled:

'Don't worry, that would be Lazarus. Right on time as usual!'

The vehicle approached us slowly and stopped. Two men jumped out and said:

'Freeze! Police! Put yuh hands in the air!'

Well boy, I nearly dead! They make Talbot and I put the casket on top of the jeep and tie it down with the ropes, then they handcuff the both of us together and lock us in the backseat. When we get to the station, they open the jeep door and took us into the charge room. Corporal Baptiste said:

'Sarge, you should ah been ah prophet, boy! Look what we have here.'

'Whey yuh get these two?' the Sergeant asked.

The Corporal said, 'Look on top the jeep.'

And when the Sergeant see the casket, he bawl:

'Jesus Christ! Beat them!'

Well Baptiste and Singh start to kick and cuff we ass all over the charge room; licks all in we head and back until finally the Sarge said to them:

'Okay, boys, that's enough! Book them and throw them in the cell. I going to take a lil sleep.'

He left the charge room.

Baptiste took down all the information and then he looked over at Singh and declared:

'Yuh eh find these fellars give we too much work for one night? Leh we cut they ass again,' and was licks like fire again.

I start to bawl:

'I want to talk to the Sergeant.'

'You want to talk to the Sergeant? Alright!' said the Corporal, taking the keys and unlocking the handcuffs from my hand. 'Walk down that corridor, you will see a door on the right. Open it and go inside, the Sergeant in there.'

I walk down the corridor, open the door but as I was going inside one, big *Alstatian* jump on me and nearly grab me by the throat. I started fighting off the dog and managed to escape and lock it back in the room. Now, I vex like that and I confront the Corporal:

'That ain't the Sergeant! That is a blasted dog you send me to get bite up with in that room.'

The Corporal laughed, 'So you calling the Sergeant ah dog now? Alright!' and he get up and walk down the corridor and knocked on the door on the left.

A puffy-faced Sergeant Doyle came out rubbing his eyes.

'Sarge,' said the Corporal, 'this gentleman say you is ah dog.'

'Beat them again,' ordered the Sergeant and they began to rain blows on us again. Then the Sergeant said, 'Enough! Now sit down let me talk to you two fellars.'

We sit down on a bench in the charge room and the Sergeant say:

'What the two of you do is the most cowardly crime that anyone can do, robbing the dead. I, personally, going to make sure that the two of you make a jail for this.'

I get frighten right away. I beg:

'Oh God, Sarge, give we ah chance nah please.'

'Chance? You disrespect my district and talking 'bout chance. *Allyuh* know what jail is? Well let me explain to you. It have seasoned prisoners in there just waiting for young fellars like the two of you to come in. They will beat you up and rough you up and bully you and some of them will even take the *y* out of the *bully* and try to do that to you also.'

I start to cry, I cold sweating, I gone down on my knees and pleading with the Sarge:

'Oh God, uncle, give we ah chance nah please.'

'Chance boy? I myself prosecuting this case to make sure the two of you make a jail.' Then he called Corporal Baptiste and said, 'Lock them in the cell,' and they pushed us in the cell and when that door slammed I swear to God I going to dead.

Twenty-past-one in the charge room, Sergeant Doyle, Corporal Baptiste and Constable Singh sit down having a chat over a cup of coffee.

'What is the age of these two fellars, Corporal?' asked the Sergeant.

Corporal Baptiste picked up the charge sheet and held it close to the light.

'The one name Talbot is twenty and the other, Frankie, is eighteen years old.'

'Pretty young fellows,' admitted the Sarge. 'Just about the same age of my two sons. Gentlemen, when I look at these two fellows, they are nothing but mere boys and somehow they don't possess the look of real criminals.'

'I share your opinion on that too,' said the Corporal.

The Sarge continued:

'I think of the whole scenario and I feel that sending these boys to jail will do more harm than good. My primary objective is to make good citizens and I think that these two boys should be given a chance. Corporal Baptiste, Constable Singh I am taking you two men into my confidence. I want you to take them both back to the Fullerton Cemetery with the casket. Let them rebury the deceased and fix things just like they were before, then take them back to Icacos and release them… and not one word of this whole episode must be uttered to anyone.'

'Good idea,' agreed Constable Singh.

'Fine by me,' concurred Corporal Baptiste.

'One more thing', said Sergeant Doyle, as he reached under the desk and came up with a bull pistle, 'I want you to keep this in the jeep and give them one each on their backs when you drop them off at Icacos.'

Corporal Baptiste chuckled:

'Sarge, you really know remedy, boy.'

Someone came and opened the door and light flooded the cell so I start to brakes one time because I sure is licks I going to get again. Baptiste and Singh took us into the charge room. The Sergeant was sitting on a chair.

'Now listen you two,' he said, 'I am going to give you all a chance.'

Well I didn't wait; I run up to the Sergeant, take off his shoes and start kissing his feet.

'Stop this foolishness before I change my mind,' demanded the Sergeant. 'Now you two will have to go back to the cemetery and straighten out the mess that you made and anytime I catch the two of allyuh in any slackness is straight to jail allyuh going.' Then he turned to the Corporal and instructed, 'You will have to hurry now, Baptiste, you don't want daylight to catch you.'

Well boy! We jump in that jeep and is speed down to Fullerton. I never see a burial happen so fast! When we finish we take all the flowers and wreaths and place them nice and orderly on the grave, and then the officers took us down to Icacos. When they stopped the vehicle, I say:

'Thank you, officers! Thank you! Allyuh could tell me the time please?'

Corporal Baptiste look at his watch and say:

'Four o'clock. But wait. Constable Singh, *ent* is police procedure to search suspects before you let them go?'

'*Jeez-an-ages*! Yes, boy, Corporal, I nearly forget that yes! The Sarge would ah vex like hell, man.' Then he turned to Talbot and me and asked politely, 'Is all right if we search you all?'

'Go right ahead, officer. No problem at all, man,' said Talbot, as we all came out of the jeep.

'Okay. Standard police procedure: hands on your heads and face the jeep,' Constable Singh said casually, like is no big deal really and he so sorry to be putting we through all the trouble, and we complied.

Something collided with Talbot back:

WHATAP!

Talbot bawl like a distressed cow and ran off into the darkness.

'Aye you! Don't run, you hear?' Corporal Singh ordered. 'Else we handcuff your arse and carry you back to the station.'

I looked to my side and I could make out the *silloette* of what seemed to be a bull pistle in Corporal Baptiste hand. He tucked it under his arm, took out a pack of cigarettes, opened it slowly, tapped one out with his forefinger and placed it in his mouth.

'You have matches, Singh?' he enquired.

Singh went over to him, took out a box of matches from his shirt pocket and lit the cigarette expertly on the first attempt. Corporal Baptiste inhaled deeply on the cigarette, slowly, deliberately, and then he blew out the smoke. He took another deep pull; I could see the lighting end of the cigarette turning to a smoldering red. He exhaled again, passed the lighting cigarette to Singh and then he walked to the back of me. I stood there, frozen, my hands on my head, my legs spread out wide, the night cool and nice but I sweating, and then suddenly I feel it:

WHATAP!

I hear men giving all sort of version about men getting hit by bull pistle and I use to think that they lie, but now? Now I know for sure they was not exaggerating. I never know I could ah run so fast. I run straight over to Emelia house and calling outside she window. Emelia say:

'Who is that?'

'Is me… Frankie,' I say.

She opened the window.

'What happen, boy? Why you twisting up you body like that?'

'Sand fly biting me,' I lied.

'Why you wake me up this hour of the morning for?' she demanded.

I gone down on my two knees in front the window and asked:

'Emelia, would you marry me?'

Emelia say:

"What is this? Some sort of joke? I hear everybody talking about you and Patsy cousin and is days now you ain't visit me."

'Emelia, I done you wrong and I sorry,' I say.

Well Emelia really love me so she asked:

'When?'

'Next week Sunday!' I blurt out.

She say:

'Nah boy… I have to invite all my family… nah… that too soon.'

'Girl, you have ah whole week!'

She scratched her head, did some calculations on her fingers and said okay.

I run home full speed to give the good news to the old people. I gone in the house and knock on their door.

The Old Man ask:

'Who is that? Frankie?'

'Yes, Old Boy, is me. I want to talk to you and mammy.'

'Now?' he asked.

I say, 'Yes now!' I hear him lighting the lamp and waking the Old Lady and when he opened the door I fly in there and hug up the two of them. 'I going to get married!'

The Old Man face take on a worried look. 'To who?' he asked.

'To Emelia,' I said.

I never see the old people so happy in my life. I leave them and gone over in my room and lie down on the bed with all my dirty clothes on, and drop off to sleep.

I got up about ten that morning and after taking breakfast, I ain't even change my clothes, I hustling over to Emelia's house to make plans for the wedding. When I passing the neighbour's house, Cindy come outside and confront me:

'You get the money?'

'Yes!'

'And where is it?' she asked.

I say:

'Girl, if I tell you something, my father gave it to me and I put it on the table and the cat eat it. If you think I lie—' and I push my hand in my pocket and pull out the piece of ten dollar note and hand it to her— 'this is all I manage to snatch from her. You could have it if you want.'

That girl start to throw a tantrum right there; she gallivanting she self, screaming:

'You Icacos fellows is ah set ah cheap sons-of-bitches! I going away from here today and I will never show my face in this village again!'

Well, I hustle out of there and gone by my Emelia.

Me and Emelia marry and we living right in the house with the old people. When I not on the fishing boats, catching my tail to make a living, I in the gallery breezing with the old people, and when I not in the gallery, I in my room romancing Emelia. Now for now we full up that house with four children, two boys and two girls. The two boys handsome just like me, but the girls just like their mother, and is a good thing, because if they did resemble me, I might ah have to pay some young boy to marry them when they come of age.

My happiest time is when I come from the sea in the afternoon and I sit down in the gallery, watching the Old Man pitching marbles with his four grandchildren in the yard and I hearing the Old Lady singing a nice hymn in the house. Then

I could hear a spoon hitting the inside of a pot and I know that my Emelia cooking something nice for the family. Is times like those that I does thank God for men like Sergeant Doyle and I does watch over by the neighbour's house, nervously hoping that Cinderella would keep she promise and never show her face in Icacos Village again.

The coffin maker

Ebennezar Trotman was born and bred in St. Vincent, a beautiful island nestled in the blue turquoise water of the Caribbean Sea. Ebennezar was a coffin builder, in fact the best on the island, and while other craftsmen were sending the general population of St. Vincent off to eternity in simple, wooden boxes, Ebennezar was experimenting, replacing square edges with curved ones and carving elaborate patterns on the lids of his coffins. Ebennezar began to get more than his fair share of business because the citizens of St. Vincent, smart people that they were, began considering the possibility that God might be giving a few marks for presentation, henceforth, going before him in an Ebennezar built coffin might afford one a much better chance of being sent to the Promised Land.

Ebennezar and his family lived in Dorsetshire, a village that stood on a hill which overlooked the capital: Kingstown. They lived quite comfortably, that is, before the arrival of Tom Brooker. Mr. Brooker lived in the same village as Ebennezar but had made off five years before to the island of Trinidad to seek his fortune. Brooker came back and told Ebennezar of an island that was flowing with milk and honey. He told him that he worked over there as an *ordinary* labourer and in five years time, he had come back with enough money to set himself up for life. Ebennezar sat there wide-eyed, smoking his pipe, listening to tales of a land where crude oil flowed through pipes and money literally grew on trees. Two weeks later, when

Brooker bought Widow Bratcher's house, Ebennezar's mind was made up. He said to his wife Marian:

"We going sell out everything and we going Trinidad to set up business, gal."

"Remember wha mammy use to always say, Ebennezar," said she. "A bird in the hand is warth two in the bush."

"Oh, you hush, gal," he said, "if that duncy head Brooker could make it over there, I reckon we kain do better."

In one month Ebennezar sold out lock, stock and barrel and bought five tickets, and his wife Marian and his three sons Isiah, Jeremiah and Jacob, and his box of tools boarded a cargo boat bound for Trinidad. When they arrived in Trinidad and came off the boat, Ebennezar sat down on his box of tools and looked at the city of Port of Spain, contemplating his next move. Same time a fellow name Gilkes passed by and Ebennezar got up and approached him. Ebennezar said:

"Good marning, Sah."

"Good morning," said Gilkes.

"Kain you tell me which part in Trinidad a man could make a good living?" asked Ebennezar.

Well Gilkes, a fisherman, who had worked in *all* the fishing villages around Trinidad, began to scratch his head, looked up at the sky, looked at Ebennezar and asked:

"You have cigarettes?"

"No. I smokes pipe," said Ebennezar.

"Well, light you pipe and give me a smoke," said Gilkes.

Ebennezar took the pipe out of his back pocket, tapped the dottle into his palm, removed a pouch from his shirt pocket and firmly packed the tobacco at the very top and about one-eighth of an inch below the top of the bowl. The first two lights, *charring lights*, involved him passing the match slowly and evenly over the top of the tobacco while he gently drew on the pipe. Gilkes waited impatiently while the tobacco blackened and the smoldering embers went out. Next, Ebennezar tamped down the tobacco that had charred and risen from the first light. Finally, he slowly and evenly lit the entire surface while drawing in deeply. Ebennezar blew out a puff of smoke and passed the pipe to him. Gilkes sucked greedily at the pipe and doubled over coughing, and then he stood up straight as an arrow, as if the coughing had given him a revelation, and said:

"Icacos man! Icacos! That is the place for you!"

"Icacos?" asked Ebennezar.

"That your family over there?" asked Gilkes.

"Yes, that is me wife and three boys."

"Well, Icacos is the place, man. No place better to raise a family and make a good living."

Gilkes gave Ebennezar directions to Icacos, tipped his hat and went his way.

Now if Gilkes had known that Ebennezar made his *living* off the dead, he would have probably advised differently because Icacos is a village where the people only eating fish and they healthy and strong as lions and does hardly ever die. Ebennezar and his family booked into a hotel in Port of Spain and the next morning at six o'clock they began the journey to Icacos. After eight hours of travelling – in three different buses – Ebennezar and entourage were dropped off in front of the Chinese shop in Icacos. They went into the shop and Ebennezar spoke to the Chinese shopkeeper who directed them to a woman named Gracie who had a small house for rent. After settling business with Gracie, Ebennezar and his family moved into the little house.

The next day Ebennezar journeyed to the hardware store in the Cedros Village and placed an order. That evening the old Bedford truck belonging to the hardware pulled up in front of the little house and offloaded galvanise and wood, for Ebennezar to build his work shed, and prime cedar boards for him to create his coffins. The following morning Ebennezar got up at five o'clock and began to build his shed and by nightfall it was completed. The next morning, he took a tin of red paint and made a sign (COFFINS MADE TO ORDER!) and nailed it up on the front post of the shed, sat down on his box of tools and began waiting for someone to die.

This became a source of great amusement to the villagers. They would pass by and read the sign and look at the tall, wiry figure, sitting there smoking his pipe, and they would hope that he had a lot of tobacco because everyone in the village knew that the last time someone had died was two years ago – that was Ma Coutou and she had died at the reasonable age of ninety one.

One month passed and nobody died; two months and still nothing doing. Ebennezar began to get worried and the amusement of the villagers soon turned to pity. The fishermen started to bring fish on a daily basis for Ebennezar and his family, and other villagers brought offerings of ground provisions and fruits.

Three months passed and the inhabitants of Icacos were still numbered among the living.

In the fourth month desperation set in. Ebennezar knelt down one night and prayed in a loud voice:

"Dear God, please let somebody die so you humble servant Ebennezar could get a work."

Marian could not believe her ears.

"Listen to youself," she reprimanded. "You ain't shame? All these things these people giving us and that is what you praying fo. I always tell ya, get a decent wark and farget them bizarre caffins that you build!"

That night the village dogs started howling in a mournful tone. Ebennezar sat up in bed.

"You hear the dogs Marian? Whenever they howl like that somebody does die."

Marian *steupsed* and turned her back to Ebennezar.

"Mark my words, gal, dogs does never lie."

The next morning there was a knocking on the Trotman's door and Ebennezar rushed out in anticipation. It was Roberts, the fish vendor who lived close to the sea.

"Good morning, Mr. Ebennezar, I came to order a coffin. My father died last night."

"I'm so sorry, Mr. Roberts. I goin come right over and measure him up," said Ebennezar.

Marian who was also now at the door shook her head in disbelief.

"Accept me sympathy, Mr. Roberts," she said and looked at Ebennezar with disdain.

Ebennezar went over and measured the dead man.

"When you want the caffin fo?" he asked.

"For tomorrow 'bout ten o'clock," replied Roberts.

Ebennezar returned home to his work shed and began sawing, cutting, carving and shaving all day and when darkness fell he lit two *flambeaus* and worked late into the night. The next morning he got up early and carved an angel with wings unto the lid of the coffin. With his job complete, he stood at a distance and looked at the coffin; it was a thing of rare beauty. That evening when they placed the coffin in the little Icacos church and the priest started his sermon, many in the congregation wished that they were dead just to be in that coffin; it was so beautiful.

The next week, a woman in the village died and the following week, an old fisherman by the name of Barsat Ali was recalled by God. Ebennezar was a busy man. Marian hardly spoke to him now as she was sure that he was in some way responsible for the sudden spate of departures to the other side; she was disgusted with Ebennezar. These good village folks had helped them along in the hard times and now her husband's prayer might be the cause of their demise.

News of Ebennezar's expertise travelled and when Darius, the big business man from Point Fortin died, his son Franklyn journeyed to the tiny village of Icacos to order a coffin.

"You have the measurements?" asked Ebennezar.

"Yes," said Franklyn and he handed Ebennezar a piece of paper.

"When you want the caffin fo?" asked Ebennezar.

"Seven o' clock tomorrow morning," said Franklin.

Ebennezar knew advertisement when he saw it and so he set out to create his greatest piece ever. He locked himself in his work shed and began. All day until late evening he worked and as darkness fell he called for his dinner, ate, lit his two flambeaus and said to Marian:

"Woman, I don't want anyone distarbing me. You understand?"

"Okay, your lardship," she said sarcastically and he returned to his work shed with his two flambeaus and locked himself in.

Ebennezar immersed himself in his work, shutting out the outside world, and the hand of the genius slowly transformed rough cedar boards into a master piece. Every now and then, he would step back from his work to look at it; he would suck on his pipe, making a bright red glow in the shed, and nod in satisfaction. Somewhere out in the night he could hear the mourning of the village dogs and he licked his lips in anticipation of another job.

Half past ten that night, Iasiah, Ebennezar's eldest son, who was nine years old, took in ill with appendicitis and Marian rushed to the work shed and called out desperately to Ebennezar.

"Woman, I tole you not to distarb me!" he shouted.

Marian ran down to the beach to Mr. Roberts who took Iasiah and her to the hospital in his fish truck. Iasiah died that night in the operating theatre.

Six o'clock the next morning, Mr. Roberts and Marian returned with the bad news and Marian's wailing brought a throng of neighbours into the yard. Ebennezar, hearing the commotion, unlocked the door and came out into the yard.

"What all you people doing here? Don't tell me you all came to arder caffins," he said.

"You wicked man!" said Marian, "Is your son Iasiah caffin they come to arder!" and she picked up an axe that was leaning against the shed and rushed Ebennezar but luckily one of the neighbours caught her in time and restrained her.

"My son Iasiah dead?" asked Ebennezar.

"Yes Ebennezar, you prayer fall on the boy too," said Marian sobbing loudly.

Ebennezar sunk to his knees and began wailing in distress. The same time Franklyn turned into the yard with a pickup truck.

"I came to collect my father's coffin," he said.

"Lawd gawd, Sah! I kain't give you that caffin," said Ebennezar.

"And why not?" asked Franklyn.

"Because my son died last night and I goin bury him in it," said Ebennezar.

"But you had a contract with me," Franklin said sternly.

"You ain't understand, Sah. I poured my soul into that there caffin. I kain't ever build another like it. Cost me mah boy so he's the one goin be buried in it," said Ebennezar.

A heated argument ensued between the two and suddenly there were loud noises coming from inside the work shed. When the neighbours looked in, Marian had used the axe and crushed the coffin into a thousand pieces.

"But what the hell is this," said Franklyn, "is mad people I dealing with!"

Ramkir, a fisherman that lived next door to Ebennezar, came to the rescue:

"Listen fellars, no sense going on like this. Way I see it we has two coffins to build. Ebennezar you have enough cedar to build them?"

"Yes," said Ebennezar.

"Darius burying today, so leh we start on he one first," said Ramkir.

And all the men in the yard went into the shed and under the guidance of Ebennezar they began cutting and sawing and shaving and within two hours they had a decent looking coffin for Darius.

"How much I owe you?" Franklyn asked Ebennezar.

"No charge," declared Ebennezar.

"No man, I must give you something." And he took out a wad of notes and placed it on the work bench and hustled off with his father's coffin.

That night, while the wake was in progress, Ebennezar was in his shed working slowly and sorrowfully on his son's coffin. By morning he was finished and they buried Iasiah that evening under a mango tree in the Fullerton cemetery. The next day Marian laid her cards on the table:

"Ebennezar, if you goin cantinue with you present type of employment I goin leave you and go back St. Vincent with my two boys."

Ebennezar had no choice. He got a job on Ramkir's boat to do fishing and he began the next week, but Ebennezar was a lousy fisherman and after one whole week he didn't catch a single fish and Ramkir said to him:

"But wait, Ebennezar, the same way you building them nice coffins, you don't think you could build a boat?"

That evening, Ebennezar went back down to the beach and had a good look at Ramkir's boat. He took out his tape measure and made some measurements, marking them down on a bit of paper. When he got home he went into his shed with a tin of paint and a piece of board. Half an hour later he came back out, took down his old sign and nailed up a new one:

BOATS BUILT TO ORDER!

And that is how the famous Trotman built pirogue boats came into being.

The elusive shoe

Toc-toc-toc.

Seuklal stared at the source of the regimented noise. It was love at first sight. The pair of *Technique* shoes, on the overseer's son's feet, magnetised Seuklal's attention. His eyes followed those shoes for the one-and-a-half mile walk from Constance Estate to the Icacos School and he didn't even feel the stones pricking at his own bare feet.

Seuklal's ambition from that day on, was to own a pair of *Techniques*. When summer holidays came, he volunteered to go into the coconut fields and work with his father, Parnalal. From sun up to sun down, he worked like a grown man alongside Parnalal. Seuklal reasoned that with the extra money, which they would make during the holidays, he would approach Parnalal to buy a pair of *Techniques* for him when school reopened. But alas, pay day after pay day the extra money that Seuklal's labour brought only meant extra drinks for Parnalal at the village's rum shop. When the holidays were over and Seuklal approached his father with his request, Parnalal flew into a rage:

'What! You wantam shoes? Better husham mouth before I puttam cutarse on you!'

Seuklal walked away dejected.

The first day of the new school term he decided not to look at the overseer's son's shoes. The *tic toc* of the shoes' soles on the hard pitch was unbearable and when the morning sun cast its rays on the shiny, black leather, the battle was lost. Seuklal's love was rekindled and when the Christmas holidays arrived he returned to the coconut fields with Parnalal. He worked even harder but his zest was properly matched by Parnalal's unquenchable thirst for rum.

The years rolled by and after Seuklal left school, at the age of sixteen, he became a full-fledged worker on the coconut estate. He saw this as his first, real chance to earn his *Techniques*. The estate paid its workers on a fortnightly basis and Seuklal began counting down the days to his salary. Unfortunately, two days before payday, tragedy struck: Parnalal died. His liver caved in to the continuous onslaught of alcohol consumption. Seuklal became the sole breadwinner in his father's house and every cent that he earned on the coconut estate was used in the sustenance of his mother, sister and three brothers. All thoughts of the *Techniques* were replaced by the struggle to keep food on the family's table.

The years rolled by and Seuklal fell in love with Indra. Eventually one of his brothers left school and started to work on the coconut estate, and the financial support of the family was now shared by both boys. Seuklal's mother decided that it was now time for his marriage and a date was fixed with the Indra's parents. The list of the wedding goodies was prepared and Seuklal counted every penny of his savings and reasoned at the end of the purchase that he might still have enough to obtain his pair of *Techniques*. But he had underestimated the prices, and at the end of the shopping there was only enough money remaining to buy a pair of rubber slippers for him to get married in. During his marriage ceremony, his attention was divided between his lovely bride and his ugly toes that were sticking out in all directions from years of walking around barefooted.

Seuklal's marriage was fruitful and the first five years produced a matching number of new mouths to be fed. At the end of ten years, he was the weary father of eight children, three girls and five boys. Seuklal's life was one of continuous toil to support his large family and the ambition of owning a *Technique* was now completely erased from his memory.

The years rolled along and the time came for Seuklal's eldest daughter, Dolly, to get married. After a suitable boy was found, and his parents had consented, a wedding date was set. One week before the wedding, the goodies list was completed and Seuklal and his wife journeyed to San-Fernando to make the purchases. When everything was secured, Seuklal still had a reasonable amount of money remaining. As they were walking along High Street, he came face-to-face with the love of his life, a pair of *Techniques*, tucked away neatly in the show room of Habibs' Shoe Store, priced nine dollars and ninety five cents, just within Seuklal's budget; he went and promptly purchased the shoe. That night, as Seuklal lay with Indra and the moon cast its luminous glow through the open bedroom window, he reached under the bed, removed the *Techniques* from its exquisite box and held it up against the pale light.

'Man,' Indra whistled, 'it lookam real nice and would makeam Dolly proud to seeam poopa wearam shoes in wedding.'

Seuklal took a piece of cloth and gently rubbed the leather.

Three days before the wedding, the guests began to arrive at Seuklal's home. One of his brothers, who lived in Penal, came with his wife, three sons and two daughters, as well as various cousins from remote villages in Trinidad, all came to help Seuklal and the family prepare for the big day.

It was an exciting time with the elders who, when they were not helping, indulged in song, dance and alcohol while the younger ones engaged in games. Two of Seuklal's nephews brought along with them their slingshots from Penal and were having a great time shooting at the numerous exotic birds that lived on the Constance Estate. Prakash, one of Seuklal's sons, eleven years at the time, was fascinated by his cousins' slingshots and begged them to make one for him. The boys had brought with them extra rubber from Penal and they cut a neat fork stick from a guava tree.

'Listen Prakash,' said the elder, 'all you have to get now is ah shoe tong.'

Prakash went into the house and started looking around for an old shoe but was unsuccessful in finding one. He then went into parents' quarters and his eyes fell on a glimmering pair. He went into the kitchen, took up the sharpest knife, came back to the bedroom, took up one of the shoes and carefully cut off the *tong*, completely ruining Seuklal's *Techniques*.

Lando

Lando took the bag from his grandmother and lifted it to his nose.

'Ah, I smell coconut bake!' he said boisterously.

'Yes my child, coconut bake and fry fish, your favorite,' replied granny.

Lando slung the bag over his shoulder and kissed his grandmother on the cheek. He stalled only for a moment and then looked at the kitchen clock; it was half-past-three in the afternoon.

'Time enough you get some nice young lady to make your bakes and give granny a rest,' she said.

'Well girl, to tell the truth ah already got my eyes on something.'

'Is she pretty?'

'As pretty as the stars in the sky.'

'Does I know her?'

'Maybe yes and maybe no,' Lando winked.

'Oh get-out-of-here, you little scoundrel you, and if you see that girl, who you say is as pretty as the stars in the sky, tell her to hurry up cause your granny is getting weary.'

'I'll see you in the morning, old girl,' he said and began walking down the road to the beach.

Janine was standing in front of her house.

'Ah boy, you going to full that boat of yours with fish tonight,' she said.

'Yep, you wanna come with me?' asked Lando.

'Who me? No, not me mister! I ain't no fisherman's woman,' said Janine, grinning mischievously.

'Where is that always late brother of yours?' asked Lando.

'He is packing his bag,' replied Janine.

Junkers came out of the house and embraced his sister. He asked:

'Tell me baby girl, is this gen'leman trying to sweet talk you or something?'

'You don't have to worry,' replied Janine, 'he can't fool me with his cunning words.'

The two men began walking towards the beach. Lando looked back, Janine waved to him and he thought: what a girl! On the shore, Lando removed his shirt and swam towards the Trotman built pirogue that was anchored in the bay. He climbed on board, aroused the Evinrude Forty Horsepower Outboard Engine, placed it in neutral, hop-skipped to the bow, hauled in the anchor and skipped back to the stern. He adjusted the engine into reverse and navigated the boat into the shallows where Junkers boarded with the bags.

The men then left Icacos behind, heading east towards the rich fishing banks, off the Erin coastline. Junkers secured the bags, then went and sat on the bow of the vessel, to serve as the lookout for oncoming boats and debris, while Lando gunned the engine towards their destination. The sun began fading from the sky and about one mile before Erin Bank, Junkers held up his hand and Lando brought the engine to a stop.

'You smell that fresh, Lando?' asked Junkers.

'Yep,' replied Lando, 'looks like we right over a school of Carite.'

'I think yuh right,' said Junkers. 'Jus head a quarter of ah mile toward the east and we will put out the net.'

Lando restarted the engine and about quarter of a mile away, they stopped. Junkers lit the lantern, that was on the buoy to mark the end of the net, and placed it in the water. They slacked off the half mile length of *filette* net – securing the end to the bow by means of a rope – and began drifting. Then, they took out their bags and shared their dinner.

By this time, night had already fallen. Junkers took out the other lantern, lit it and placed it on the pole at the stern of the pirogue. Lando took the old West Clock out of his bag and set the alarm for ten o'clock, and then they lay in the open boat to catch some shuteye until the prehistoric timepiece blared. Lando was restless. He kept tossing and turning.

'Something wrong lil brother?' asked Junkers.

'Yep,' said Lando, 'something heavy on my mind.'

'How heavy?'

'Real heavy, boy, Junkers.'

'Anything I could help with?'

'I don't know how this would go down with you, man,' Lando said.

'Try me.'

'Well… me an you have lived like brothers since we small an I have always considered Janine like my lil sister.'

'And that is how it should be,' Junkers cut in.

'But lately I've… I've been getting some feelings for she,' said Lando.

'What sort ah feelins?'

'Well, yuh know nah… I think… I think I'm in love with her,' Lando admitted.

Junkers reached into his bag, took out his knife, grabbed Lando by his hair and pressed the blade against his throat.

'Listen young fellar,' he warned, 'you leave my blasted sister alone. Since my father died I've spent every cent I make to send her to school. Now she pass all her subjects and she have two more years to do her advance. So stop feeling your blasted feelings for the next two years and then you could come back and talk to me then.'

'Easy Junks, easy. I get you point.'

39

'I done talk,' said Junkers, releasing the grip he had on Lando's hair.

Captain Roel Vanslightman had left the Essequibo River onboard The Guyana Star, a two-hundred-and-fifty-foot steel hull cargo vessel, with a full load of rice and lumber bound for Port of Spain, Trinidad. The Guyana Star was now off the coast of Moruga and Captain Vanslightman himself was at the helm; reason being: an unusual amount of filette vessels were fishing off the coast of Moruga. It was quite difficult to maneuver between the vessels without cutting the long nets that they drifted off their bows but the captain, who was a fisherman in his youth, was very careful when passing between these fishing boats, for he knew the expenses the fisher folks would incur should his vessel run over their nets. Every now and then, Bartica, who was the duty lookout, would talk-sing: 'Light off the starboard bow, Cappy!' or 'Light off the port bow, Cappy!' and Captain Vanslightman would alter his course to ensure the safe passage from the fishermen and their nets.

They were approaching the Erin banks, and had now passed the majority of fishing boats. The captain decided it was time to go in and take a rest and he sent Bartica to summon the first mate and the new lookout. First Mate Ralston Oliverrie was a drinking man and although Captain Vanslightman never allowed liquor on the vessel, he always managed to smuggle a few bottles onboard before leaving Guyana. Tonight, the first mate and the men were secretly passing the bottle and when Bartica entered the room, Oliverrie and the new lookout, Capstan, had already consumed an enormous amount of alcohol. When Oliverrie and Capstan entered the wheelhouse, they made sure and kept their distance from the captain, for they did not want him to smell the alcohol on their breath. Captain Vanslightman briefed them about the fishing boats and upon handing over, retired to his quarters. Fresh breeze, from a westerly wind, was blowing through the open door of the wheelhouse and within minutes Capstan and Oliverrie were nodding on themselves.

The Guyana Star sailed unmanned into the darkness.

Junkers awoke, flicked on his torchlight and looked at the West Clock: it was nine thirty, half an hour away from pulling in the net. He looked at Lando sleeping and knew that his friend did not have any bad intentions but it was just a case of bad timing; two years bad timing. He was going to awaken him but decided to allow him the extra *half-an-hour* sleep. He lit a cigarette and sat on the bow of the boat smoking, contemplating his altercation with Lando. Clearly, he had been too harsh on his friend, but as soon as he awoke he would apologise to him. Lando turned on his side and coughed.

'You up, boy?' asked Junkers.

'Yes man, but ah had a funny sort of dream.'

'What you dream, boy?'

'I dream that the both of us was in a garden and a lot of ants come and surround you and suddenly these thousands ants turn to angels and start to fly all around you.'

Junkers replied:

'That ain't no funny sort of dream, man, that is a good dream. Them thousands of ants you dream about is really the amount of fish we going to ketch in that net tonight.'

'And what about the angels?'

'Them is the ones that guiding the fish into the net,' said Junkers.

'Okay.'

'And, by the way, I want to apologise to you about earlier. Give her a little time and let her concentrate on her school work and after I'll be proud to have you as my brother-in-law... now let we get that net and it is fish for so in the boat.'

Lando smiled.

They moved their sleeping bags from the centre of the boat and secured them beneath the bow then Lando held on to the main sheet rope and dragged it until he had the net in his hand. He passed the lead line to Junkers and he held on to the cork line and they began to heave it in. Within two minutes they began to get fish entangled in the net.

'There is a big Carite!' Junkers shouted. 'And there is another!'

'Whey! Look at fish!' Lando exclaimed, as Carite appeared by the dozens.

'We going to murder them tonight!' shouted Junkers as he untangled another fish and threw it into the boat.

'Junkers, you really know how to interpret dream, boy!' shouted Lando.

Junkers laughed and began singing the Mighty Sparrow's *Ten to one is murder* at the top of his voice and Lando joined in with his rusty voice as they pulled in Carite after Carite. Junkers sang at the top of his voice:

'*And… it was licks like fire but they wouldn't surrender…*'

'*Ten to one is murder,*' Lando chorused in his rusty baritone, as he bent over to untangle another fish.

It was Junkers who heard it first. He looked to his right and saw the big steel monster meters away, its green and red eye looking down at them, and Junkers' calypso was lost in mid verse–

'Jump Lando, jump!' he shouted, as he himself dived over board.

The Guyana Star ploughed into the wooden pirogue and crushed it into pieces and Lando got caught in the impact and was violently flung into the sea.

'Lando! Lando!'

'Over here! Over here!'

Junkers swam towards the voice.

'You get lash boy?' he asked.

'Yeah man,' grunted Lando, 'I think I busted one of my ribs.'

'Oh hell! Hold on to me. We have to paddle around to see if we could find piece of debris to cling to.'

After five, frantic minutes they happened upon a shattered bit of the pirogue; it was a solid bit, made up of boards nailed together on three braces or ribs, about six feet by four.

'Now hold on, padner,' said Junkers, 'I have to try to get you on top this piece of wreckage.'

Lando winced with pain but finally Junkers managed to place him on his back on the piece of wreckage.

'How you feeling, boy?' asked Junkers.

'I feel like something piercing my inside,' groaned Lando.

'Okay man, you stay quiet, I'm right here with you,' said Junkers.

Mercifully the sea was calm but there was room for only one person on the piece of wreckage so Junkers just held on to the side and drifted along; the current was heading in a westerly direction, pushing them back down to Icacos.

'Junkers, I am sorry about what I told you earlier on,' Lando said in a painful voice.

'Don't worry about that, boy,' Junkers said, searching the waters intensely, looking for a light. 'Try and stay quiet so you won't aggravate the pain.'

Lando began trembling violently. Junkers took off his shirt, wrung the water out of it and covered Lando. They drifted along for a while and Junkers saw a light.

"Lando, ah seeing a light, boy! 'Bout ah mile down."

As the light drew closer, Junkers started paddling with his foot to try to get the wreckage as close as possible. It was a fishing boat but they were about seventy metres away. Junkers could make out the shape of the vessel below the dim light of the lantern and he started shouting in a loud voice and paddling with his foot but there was no response. They were now within sixty metres of the boat, but that was the closest they would get for already the current was pushing them downstream. Junkers continued bawling and yelling at the top of his voice, but no one heard his cries. Already they were out of earshot of the boat. Junkers cursed his bad luck, and then he comforted Lando:

'Don't worry, partner… the next one will hear us.'

They drifted all night and never came close to another vessel. When dawn broke Junkers could see the Icacos point about five miles below them. Lando was drifting in and out of consciousness. Junkers noticed streaks of blood at the corners of his mouth.

'Lando, yuh hearing me boy?' asked Junkers, but there was no reply.

Junkers searched the waters looking for a boat but it was Sunday morning and there was no one leaving the village to go fishing. Junkers unbuttoned the front of Lando's shirt: the right side of his rib cage was black and blue and he was running a high fever. Junkers took scoops of water in his hand and began rubbing it on the face and body of Lando, trying to lower the fever. Lando started to mutter something about his grandmother.

'Easy brother… easy,' said Junkers.

About nine o'clock that morning, when Junkers and Lando drifted past Icacos, they were about three-and-a-half miles off the coast, close enough to see the roofs of the houses that were nearer to the sea. Junkers began waving in earnest, hoping that someone would see them but he knew that at that distance it was impossible. From time to time he could feel little fishes nibbling at his feet but he busied himself anointing Lando with water. He could see blood bubbles forming around Lando's nostrils.

'Hold on little brother, hold on,' he pleaded. 'Remember Janine is waiting for you boy, you don't have to worry, you know. You could come around after school in the evening and visit her. You could take her cinema on the weekend… you could even steal a little kiss in the cinema.' Junkers almost chuckled. 'I will not vex. You understand boy? You got to hold on.'

The midday sun burned down on the two men with a vengeance and Junkers had to continually soak the face and body of Lando who was muttering something about his granny again.

'Listen pardner,' said Junkers, 'is about twelve o'clock now, they would know something wrong. They probably launching the search vessel right now, you got to hold on.'

Junkers looked down into the water he could still see the little fishes nibbling at his feet, but funny… he was not feeling anything.

'Lando boy,' he said, 'you know them two cows that I have? Well when Janine finish school and you two going to get married, I going to sell them two cows and rent one of them big limousines to carry the wedding.'

But there was no reply.

He was so busy tending to Lando that he didn't even notice it; without warning, the cramps overtook Junkers' legs and dissipated into his upper body. Soon he was having trouble holding on to the wreckage and suddenly he lost his grip and down he went; down, down, down… down into Davy Jones' locker.

The search party found Lando drifting on the wreckage three o'clock that afternoon. They rushed him to shore, took him to Point Fortin Hospital by car and then he was transferred by ambulance to the San Fernando Hospital where he spent two months.

The villagers kept on searching for Junkers but they never found him.

When Lando was released from hospital, he secured a job with the Ministry of Works. He used his salary to send Janine to school and to maintain his granny and himself. Two years later, Janine graduated with full passes in her advanced exams. She got a job as a teacher and, one month later, she and Lando got married in a simple ceremony on the Icacos beach, both bride and groom looking out to sea and exchanging their vows with teary eyes.

Somewhere in that watery expanse, a departed would have found some solace.

The fight of the century

The Icacos shop was quiet in the blazing afternoon sun. Ping, the Chinese shopkeeper, was at the scale scooping split peas from a crocus bag and weighing them into one pound bags. Beads of perspiration rolled down his forehead, unto his once white, sleeveless merino. Arthur, his son, sat in a rocking chair reading the newspaper from the day before. Every now and then, he would take a scissors out of his pocket, cut out a picture or an article from the newspaper and place it neatly into a box. Arthur was Ping's only child and when his mother had died, when he was only ten, Ping had resigned himself to tending shop and raising him.

They were a rare combination. Ping did all the work and Arthur did all the reading and observing. During the day he would pass on pieces of information, he had read or observed, which he thought might be of interest to Ping. Arthur had simple daily routines. He would get up at five o'clock in the morning, feed his many caged birds, and then he would sit in the rocking chair and look out for the six o'clock bus. Four buses arrived at Icacos from Point Fortin on a daily basis: one at six, one at nine, one at two and the other at six in the afternoon. Arthur rarely ever missed the stop of one of these buses. They stopped and turned directly in front of the shop and the passengers for the tiny village of Icacos would get off here.

Arthur took great pleasure observing the people that came off the buses. They came from all parts of Trinidad and even other islands of the West Indies; fishing was the main thing that drew them. Arthur would study their faces as they came off the bus and try to label them one by one: fishing, fishing, come to look for family, fishing, breaking warrant, fishing. He was hardly ever wrong.

Ping weighed out the last parcel of split peas and sighed. A heavy rumbling was coming down the road and shortly after, the two o'clock bus pulled up in front of the shop. Arthur lowered the newspaper and fixed his eyes on the door of the bus. There was only one passenger, a man dressed in a blue shirt and black, baggy pants. He came off the bus and walked into the shop.

'Good afternoon, gents,' he said.

'Goo aftelnoon,' replied Ping.

'Sir, can I have two cigarettes and a drink of your strongest rum?' asked the stranger.

Arthur was sure he had seen that face before.

Ping gave the stranger the cigarettes, reached for the bottle of Puncheon Rum and poured a drink into a glass. The stranger took up the glass, said 'cheers', tossed the liquor down his throat and twisted his face, clearly underestimating the strength of the rum.

Arthur was amused.

'Would you gen'lemen know where a body could get a room to rent?' asked the stranger, composing himself.

'Well, if is fishing you came to do,' said Arthur, 'you can speak to one of the boat owners and they wid put you up in one of the shacks along the beach… free of charge.'

'Thank you, Sir,' replied the stranger.

'What did you say your name was?' asked Arthur.

'Never said,' replied the stranger, as he walked out of the shop.

Arthur got up from the rocking chair and looked at the stranger as he made his way towards the beach. Now where had he seen that face before?

Ten o'clock that night Ping was trying to sleep but Arthur was pacing the floor of the bedroom.

'Wha the matter Ata?' asked Ping, but Arthur did not answer. 'Wha happin Ata, you want to get mallied? Just tell Papa if you want to get mallied. I light letter light now to China and Tanty Nolla send nice, pletty, pletty Chiney gir for you to mally. Eh, Ata?'

Arthur was impatient. 'I don't want to marry yet, Papa! I am thinking!'

'Tinkin?' said Ping. 'You walk up and down and say tinkin? Man no tink with foot.'

'I know Papa, I am walking and thinking,' said Arthur.

Ping *steupsed*. 'Time for Ping to play with gland chillen and twenty-four-year-old man walkin an tinkin in middle of nite.'

Arthur left the bedroom and went into the shop area. He took a bubble gum out of a glass jar, peeled off the paper, popped it into his mouth and started chewing. He took the gas lamp down from its hook and started pumping it with air, then he raised the glass and lit the mantle. The gas lamp roared to life and flooded the shop with light. Arthur returned to the bedroom. Ping was now asleep. He looked at the old man and smiled, then he took a blanket and covered him. He reached below the bed and took out the three boxes of newspaper clippings and pictures he had horded over the years. Arthur took the boxes one by one into the shop area and started sorting through them. There was a picture of Eric Williams, a picture of Joe Louis and an article about Mahatma Gandhi. He went on sorting: a picture of Buzz Butler, an article about the Queen of England. On and on he went until he emptied the first box. Into the second box he went: a picture of Sir Winston Churchill, an article about Sir Edmund Hillary, and midway through that second box… bingo! Arthur had in his hand a large picture of a man in boxing gloves and shorts, with a screaming headline:

'BAJAN PUGILIST ROBBED IN WORLD TITLE FIGHT!'

Arthur held up the picture against the light, looking at it carefully, and then he began reading the article:

'*Barbadian boxer Bill Barnes pummeled the American welter weight champion for fifteen rounds in a New York Arena, yet the referee raised the hand of the bruised and battered American in victory after the fight. The crowd booed and threw objects into the ring after the decision, which clearly was won by the Bajan.*'

Arthur could hardly contain himself. He lifted the picture to the light again but there was no mistaking; the man in the picture and the stranger who got off the two o'clock bus were one and the same. He extinguished the gas lamp, went into the room, quietly climbed into bed beside his father and fell asleep.

The next morning, Arthur fed his birds and took up his position in the rocking chair, but this time he wasn't looking for the bus, he was looking at the road leading to the beach to see when the stranger would make an appearance. He had to wait a long time, for the stranger had already gone fishing on one of the boats, and it was at five o'clock in the afternoon when he sauntered into the shop. Arthur rushed behind the counter to attend to him.

'One nip of rum, a pound of rice, a pound of split peas and a half pound of salt meat,' requested the stranger.

Arthur prepared the items, placed them in a bag and collected his money. The stranger picked up the bag and as he was walking through the door Arthur exclaimed:

'Bill Barnes!'

The stranger spun around.

Arthur knew he had him.

The stranger came back to the counter and demanded:

'Speak!'

Arthur took the picture out of his pocket and unfolded it in the stranger's face.

The stranger looked at the picture and pursed his lips. 'Okay… you got me.'

Arthur smiled. It was Bill Barnes indeed, the former world welter weight boxing contender who was twice robbed in world title fights. Frustrated and broken of spirit, he quit boxing and began drifting from place to place. He came to Trinidad and now at age thirty seven and almost an alcoholic, found himself in the tiny fishing village of Icacos.

Arthur stretched to the top shelf and took down a bottle of his finest liquor and placed it on the counter. He then brought two glasses and a bottle of water. Breaking the seal of the bottle, he passed it to the Bajan who threw a generous helping into his glass. Arthur poured some into his own glass, the Bajan toasted cheers and both men threw the liquor down their throats. Arthur twisted his face.

'Not a drinkin man?' asked the Bajan.

'Nope,' replied Arthur.

'Then why did you drink it?' asked the Bajan.

'In honor of a great champion,' said Arthur.

The Bajan smiled. They took another drink and then Arthur gave Bill the bottle.

'What's this?' asked the Bajan.

'On the house,' said Arthur.

'Listen,' Barnes asked, 'could we keep my identity a secret?'

'Impossible!' said Arthur.

'How do you mean?' asked Barnes.

'Do you know what this would mean to the people of this little village?' asked Arthur. 'Having a man of your calibre among them would provide great inspiration to everyone. So do you think that we should deny them this opportunity?'

'Well, looking at it from that angle… I suppose you have a point.'

Arthur spread the word quickly and effectively and by the next day, everyone knew of the great boxer's presence. Bill Barnes was a celebrity once again, with the villagers pampering him everywhere he went.

'You sure know how to set up a man,' said Barnes to Arthur the next day when he visited the shop.

Arthur smiled. 'So what do you think of the village?'

'Piece of heaven man,' said Barnes.

'You planning to stay a while?' asked Arthur.

'Doubt if I will ever leave,' replied the Bajan.

Barnes settled into the village and two months after his arrival, Arthur came up with an idea because he continually fantasised about seeing the Bajan fight. Why not promote a fight between Barnes and one of the villagers? He picked up a writing pad and pencil and began to pace the floor – Ping, who was bottling cooking oil from a drum, looked at him from head to toe and sighed.

Arthur was marking names on the pad and crossing them off as he moved to and fro. He was trying to come up with a suitable opponent to face off with the Bajan. He had first marked the name Joseph on the pad. Joseph was a big strong fellow from St. Lucia but he was very slow; he would be easy to corner and would not last long with Barnes. Arthur scratched his name from the pad. Then he came up with Baker, a Tobagonian who Arthur knew was a good fighter from the many brawls he had witnessed in the rumshop. He scratched off his name also because he remembered that Baker would use anything that came into his hands to defeat an opponent and he didn't want this match to turn into a fiasco. At the end of the exercise, he had the name *Mystery Kid* marked on the pad.

Sonilal Preston, also known as the *Mystery Kid*, was fit as a fiddle and agile as a monkey. He had a good physique because he was always taking exercises and moreover he was only eighteen and had the energy, Arthur thought, to perhaps stay with Barnes for a round or two. Arthur smiled. All he had to do now, was soften up Ping to get the permission to stage the fight. He placed the notebook and pencil on the counter. Ping had completed filling another bottle of oil and was wiping the outside of the bottle with an old, greasy cloth.

'Okay Ata, wat de ploblem?' asked Ping.

'Oh just thinking…' said Arthur.

'Tinkin wha?' asked Ping.

'Well I know how you always talking about grandchildren.'

Ping put the bottle of oil on the shelf and hastily pulled up a chair.

'You want me lite letter light now to Tanty Nolla?' he asked.

'Oh no, no Papa,' replied Arthur. 'I already have a girl!'

'Aleady have gir?' asked Ping.

'Yes Papa. I already have a girl. Daisy, Miss Melda's daughter.'

Ping looked up at his son and smiled. 'You sly poy, al time have nice, pletty pletty douglin gir hide away and no tell Papa notin?'

Arthur shrugged.

Ping's eyes were bright. 'Ata poy, you know Daisy mama Indian, an papa neglo, an you mama Indian and you Papa chiney. Many laces make many, pletty, pletty gland chillen.'

Ping became a happy man. Whenever he passed Arthur during the day, he would chuckle and slap him on the back, saying:

'You sly poy.'

In the afternoon Arthur raised the matter with Ping telling him about his plans to stage the fight.

'Oh go light ahead, poy, no ploblem,' said Ping, slapping him on the shoulder. 'You know Ata, shop only ha one bedloom, have to contac calpenter fella name Moscow to puild odder bedloom for you and Taisy, for Papa no want to see tecnical part of making glanchillen.'

Arthur laughed heartily; his father said the funniest things sometimes.

Arthur now had two missions: firstly, to get both men to agree to the fight and secondly, to work on his relationship with Daisy. He believed that he and Daisy had something going; it was more like an invisible sort of thing because he had never really spoken to her about it. But it was there, the way she smiled at him when she came into the shop and she always brought him sweets when she made. Why, the best sugarcake and fudge he had ever tasted were Daisy's. But seriously, supposing he was reading the signals wrong? Maybe she just liked him as a friend, and he had already gone and run his mouth off to Ping. Arthur was worried. He could not be wrong… he had seen how those dark eyes had looked at him from time to time. There was something between them, but they were both too shy to communicate their feelings. Arthur would have to work on this. Tomorrow morning he would journey down to the beach to speak to Bill Barnes and Sonial Preston.

Arthur awoke early and fed his birds. He was nervous. He was accustomed to dealing with the fishermen from behind a counter, but now he had to go into their domain. He pondered at his nervousness and then realised how sheltered his life had been, why he hardly ever ventured out of the shop. Yes he was friends with all the fishermen, why, he always gave them *trust* when things were hard and the occasional free drink of rum, he even gave them free groceries if they came with a credible story, but he had never been on their turf, those three hundred yards of beach front with its numerous little crude shacks that they referred to as the *ranch*; that carnival strip where men were housed to go to sea. Arthur knew the ranch from a distance when he walked his birds, the sight of bareback men cooking over open fires and the countless lines straining under laundered colourful clothes. He had heard many tales of the gambling and fighting that took place down there, of men who toiled hard all day, then gambled and drank away their day's earnings, fought with each other, then got up as brothers the next morning, sharing their rations and sailing out in their fishing boats as if nothing had happened.

Arthur felt inferior to them. They were a rare breed of independent men, sea dogs if ever there were. He had to go down there. Psyching himself, he picked up one of his birdcages and walked down to the beach. There were at least a dozen fires where men were cooking and getting ready to go to sea. A Tobagonian fellow, by the name of Snake, was frying fish in front of the first hut.

'Aye Atar, wha you doin in dis part o' the world, marn?' he asked.

'Looking for Bill Barnes and Sonilal,' replied Arthur.

'Well not befo you try a piece o' me fry fish,' said Snake, scooping out a large slice of Cavali from the pot, placing it on a piece of banana leaf and handing it to him.

Arthur tried it. It was tasty, hot, but very tasty.

'Good eh?' asked Snake.

'Yep, really good,' remarked Arthur.

'Now bout them two son of a bitches, wha hapin they owe you money?'

'No, no,' replied Arthur, 'just wanted to talk to them.'

'Oright, Sanilal garn out to sea a'ready but Barnes by de hut whey de blue blanket hangin pon de line.'

Arthur thanked Snake but had to taste at least three more pots on his way to Barnes. It was amazing, the hospitality of these fishermen. Barnes was brewing coffee in a tin cup over a small fire.

'Good morning, Sir, what a pleasant surprise,' he said.

'Morning Champ, wanted to have a few words with you,' said Arthur.

'Gotta be quick words,' said Barnes, 'cause we will be sailing shortly.'

'Okay, in a nutshell,' said Arthur, 'I want to stage a boxing match.'

'With whom?' asked Barnes.

'You and Sonilal,' said Arthur.

'Madness! Complete madness!' said Barnes.

'Listen,' said Arthur, 'there is something in this for both of you. Why don't you and Sonilal pass by the shop this afternoon and hear what I have to say?'

'Okay,' said Barnes, and Arthur went back to the shop.

Arthur spent the rest of the day formulating words which he hoped would convince both men to accept the fight. When they came to him, about six that afternoon, he was ready. Sonilal didn't need much convincing; he was looking for an opportunity to showcase his strength and physical prowess. Bill Barnes wanted no part of it. Arthur began to launch a diplomatic attack:

'Listen Champ, think about the positive influence this fight will have on the young people of the village.'

Barnes stuck his forefinger into his chest and scoffed, 'You want me to get into a ring–' he pointed at Sonilal– 'with a little boy who has never put on a boxing glove in his life?'

'Like you never hear bout David and Goliath?' cut in Sonilal.

'Well Champ, Sonilal ain't exactly a boy and besides this is a good opportunity to inject some life into the village,' Arthur inveigled.

In the end Barnes gave in and the terms and conditions were ironed out. The fight would be fifteen rounds, each round three minutes long. It would take place in two months and Arthur would provide both men with a sum of money, so that they wouldn't have to work and could use the time leading up to the fight exclusively for training. The winner would receive a whooping one-hundred-and-twenty-five dollar prize, a gallon of cask wine and a bottle of Puncheon Rum, while the loser would claim fifty dollars and a bottle of Puncheon Rum.

Sonilal Preston lay awake late that night thinking. He had never known his mother. The way he heard it, his mother was a prostitute who came to Icacos once a month to hustle the fishermen. She disappeared for some time and then, without warning, turned up one day, cradling a little baby boy in her arms. She waited until dusk, when all the fishermen had returned from the sea, and once they had congregated around her in a claustrophobic circle, she wagged a disapproving finger at each and inveighed:

'One of you son-of-a-bitches is de fadda ah dis chile!'

'Listen, Teresa, you have to be more specific,' said David Nottingham, a learned fisherman from San Fernando who was chilling out in Icacos.

'Spe-fic my ass,' said Teresa. 'All ah you do ting, so all ah you play part. Now all ah you go get a chance to play daddy.'

And with that she placed the child on the ground and stormed away, never to be seen again. Well, a lot of confused looking fishermen stand up on the Icacos beach and when Snake reach down and pick up the infant, he gave a pretty, little smile and break all the fishermen hearts. The end result was the fishermen took the baby to a woman named *Tan Tan*, who lived by herself near the beach, and they pooled up money on a weekly basis to pay her for his upkeep. Tan Tan named the baby Sonilal Preston since his mother's name was Teresa Preston, but everyone just called him the *Mystery Kid*. Tan Tan raised Sonilal properly, sending him to school and taking him to church on Sundays.

Sonilal grew into a strong and athletic child. When he was fourteen years old Tan Tan died. Sonilal quit school and went to live in one of the shacks on the *ranch* and became a fisherman. He was fed up of looking at every fisherman and trying to see if there was any resemblance. Could this one be his father? Or maybe it was that one!

This fight was going to give him an identity; he was going to be known as the *man* who cut Bill Barnes ass good and proper or he was going to die trying.

Sonilal awoke at four thirty the next morning and brewed his tea. After drinking a full cup, he set out on an early morning run along the Icacos beach. He ran almost four miles and returned to his hut about six o'clock. The fishermen were preparing to go to sea.

'What happen kid? You ain't working today?' asked Moonwah, the owner of the boat on which Sonilal worked.

'Boss-man, I was meaning to talk to you, ah need to get two months off,' said Sonilal.

'What happen, you going to get married?' Moonwah joked to the laughter of the other fishermen who were moving around.

'Nah, going to fight Barnes. I need two months to train.'

'What!' exclaimed Moonwah 'You know what you doing? Bill Barnes beat the best of the best, boy. You getting mad or something?'

'Listen, I ask you for two months off. You giving me or not?' asked Sonilal.

'Suit yourself, young boy,' said Moonwah and so it was the news of the pending battle was released on the people of Icacos.

Bill Barnes went out to sea as usual but Sonilal stayed at home and began to put things in place for the next two months. First, he went to the shop and bought groceries: rice, salted meat and peas – lots and lots of peas – and other miscellaneous items. Arthur placed the items in a cardboard box and Sonilal requested an empty crocus bag.

'An empty crocus bag?' Arthur queried.

'Yep. I am gonna fill that up wit sand and use it as a punching bag,' said Sonilal.

'Bright start, kid… bright start,' said Arthur.

Sonilal went home and after storing his groceries, he proceeded to half fill the empty crocus bag with sand, then he tied it with a rope and slung it over a branch of the almond tree that grew behind his shack.

The next morning, Sonilal rose at half-past-four and after having his tea, he proceeded to beat the daylights out of the bag of sand. At six o'clock he ran for one hour on dead sand and then at seven o'clock he went for a long swim. After drying himself, he lit his fire and put up his peas with a piece of salted meat to boil, then he threw in some rice, making a sort of *peleau*. When he was finished cooking, he sat down and ate heartily. Then he retired to his hammock and fell soundly asleep. He got up at twelve sharp and ate the remaining food. At four o'clock in the afternoon, he picked up a cylindrical log he had found on the beach; it was four feet long, nine inches in diameter and forty pounds, give or take a few. He placed it on his shoulder and proceeded to walk one mile back and forth along the beach. After securing the log, he went into the sea and had a good soak. At six in the afternoon, he ate fish broth with his fellow fishermen, and this became the day-to-day routine of Sonilal Preston for the next two weeks.

Arthur also began his preparations for the fight. Ten days after the date was announced, he called in both men and measured their feet. The next day he journeyed to San Fernando and went to a sports store. He purchased a red pair of boxing gloves, red boxing shorts with white trimmings, and a red pair of boxing boots for Sonilal. Then he bought a black pair of boxing gloves, black boxing shorts with white trimmings, and a black pair of boxing boots for Barnes.

'Anything else?' asked the clerk.

'Yep,' replied Arthur, 'two mouth guards.'

After he paid for and collected his items, he went to High Street and bought some white sleeveless merinos for Ping. Then he bought a large chocolate and a bunch of roses and boarded a bus to return to Icacos. When he reached home he gave the merinos to Ping and placed the boxing gear under the bed. He secured the chocolate and placed the roses in a jar of water.

Daisy came into the shop the next morning and Arthur was ready with gifts and words. He gave her the chocolate and she smiled. He went into the room for the flowers (they had withered a bit) and brought them to Daisy.

'These have withered but yesterday they looked beautiful just like you,' he said.

Daisy was thrilled.

After fourteen days of rigorous training Sonilal took a day off. He just loafed around, took a bath in the sea and then relaxed in his hammock. Around two in the afternoon he went over to the shop and purchased some more supplies. Arthur gave him two more empty crocus bags and said:

'Wonder if you and Bill Barnes could check me around six this afternoon?'

'Okay,' said Sonilal and he left with his goods.

When Barnes came in from fishing Sonilal told him of Arthur's wishes and they both went to see him at six o'clock. Arthur was waiting. He had a big, black bag on the counter.

'Got something to show you fellows,' he said and started to take the equipment out of the bag.

Sonilal's eyes lit up. He took a pair of the boots, held it up to his face and kissed it, then he looked over at Bill Barnes and ran his index finger across his throat in a cutthroat sign. Bill Barnes smiled. Arthur said:

'Sonilal, you'll be fighting in the red outfit with white trimmings and Barnes will be fighting in black with white trimmings.'

Sonilal resumed training the next morning and when Bill Barnes peeped through his back window, he noticed that the kid was actually bursting holes in the new bag of sand with his punches. Barnes was impressed, even apprehensive, and he stayed home that day and began his own training, starting off with a mile run and a short swim. That evening, Arthur placed the equipment on display. The villagers filed in to get a look at genuine boxing gloves and boots. They wanted to feel them, to touch them, but Ping said sternly:

'Watch! But no touch!'

The excitement was really building up. The next day Arthur called in both men and weighed them on the big shop scale which was used for weighing large items. Barnes weighed in at one hundred and forty-seven pounds and Sonilal came in at one hundred and forty one pounds. Arthur then took a marker and made three posters:

FIGHT OF THE CENTURY

Sunday 25th August 1958

Featuring:

Bill Barnes
ex No. 1 World Welter Weight Contender

Vs

Sonilal '*Mystery Kid*' Preston
Ambitious teenager

Venue: *In Front Ping's Shop, Icacos*

He stuck one up in Icacos, one in the village of Fullerton and one in Cedros. The excitement was spreading beyond the boundaries of Icacos.

Ex-British R.A.F. Serviceman John Collins who had settled in Cedros saw the poster and started making inquiries. He found the young teenager who was going to do battle with Bill Barnes, training his heart out on the Icacos beach. Collins flew fighter planes in the Second World War and had become a boxing instructor with the R.A.F. before retiring. He offered his assistance to Sonilal and he accepted. A new program was put in place: Sonilal continued to rise early, taking his early morning runs and swims and punching his sandbag, but every evening he caught a taxi and journeyed to Cedros where Collins taught him the fine art of boxing. Collins introduced him to an arsenal of weapons: the uppercut, left hook, short jab and body punches. He taught him how to execute them correctly and use them effectively to hurt an opponent. He taught him lateral movement, how to evade punches, how to use both fists to cover his head when hurt and the importance of combination punching. He lectured him on pacing himself and conserving energy during the fight.

'And don't forget the killer instinct, my boy, you hurt him you finish him,' he said.

When Sonilal worked the punching bag on mornings, he practised the shots that Collins taught him. When Barnes saw this he was amazed. He had already stepped up his own training but now he was taking no chances; he stopped drinking alcohol and began preparing himself as if he was going into a big one. Two weeks before fight time, the combatants were really at it. Both men had intensified their training, Barnes now had his own punching bag and a large crowd of villagers would gather on mornings to watch him go through his routine. They especially liked to see his slick brand of skipping which Barnes did with such speed that one hardly saw the rope he used. Both men avoided each other as much as possible.

Meanwhile, Arthur was busy tying up loose ends. One week before fight time he brought in the Carpenter fellow, Moscow, to build the ring. Moscow took his axe and went into the Icacos mangrove swamp, where he cut four, solid mangrove posts and when he returned, he measured the dimensions of a boxing ring in front of the shop and planted these four posts.

Arthur then brought out a new coil of three-quarter-inch rope which Moscow used to fence the ring.

The next day, Moscow journeyed to Fullerton, where he bought four crocus bags of fibre from the fibre factory. This he used, together with strips of cloth from flour bags, to pad the four mangrove posts of the ring. Arthur then borrowed a tractor and trailer from the Constance Coconut Estate and he brought in a trailer of the finest sand to spread in the ring. When Moscow was finished, Icacos had its own version of a boxing ring and even Barnes nodded his approval.

One day before the fight, Arthur brought in both boxers for a public weigh in and a large crowd gathered outside the shop to witness the affair. Barnes came in at one hundred and forty-three pounds and Sonilal, one hundred and forty. Arthur announced that the referee, three judges and a cornerman would be coming from Point Fortin, all knowledgeable men in boxing. The Point Fortin Cornerman would work with Bill Barnes and John Collins would serve as the cornerman for Sonilal

It was four-fifteen in the afternoon, Sunday the 25th of August, 1958. Men, women, children, dogs, caged birds and transient cows and goats had packed the area around the ring, in front of the shop. People spilled into the road and men climbed into trees and onto Ping's roof. The crowd was huge and the atmosphere was electrifying.

The fighters came into the ring, looking like gladiators, muscles glistening in the afternoon sun; the crowd roared its approval. The referee introduced the fighters:

'In the left corner, fighting with red boots, red shorts and red gloves... Sonilalllllllllllll Preston! And in the right corner, wearing black boots, black shorts and black gloves... Billlllllllllllll Barnes!'

Then he took a piece of paper out of his pocket and read the rules of the fight.

The coconut estate time keeper, a fellow named Bisram, who was given the job of bell man, looked up at the huge clock that Arthur had hung on a pole and as it struck four-thirty, he clanged the school bell to start the fight of the century.

The Kid bolted out of his corner like a tiger, completely surprising the older man. He unleashed a barrage of blows and Barnes had to cover up. The crowd went wild! The Kid continued punching away and suddenly Barnes sneaked out an upper cut that caught The Kid on the chin, visibly stunning him. The Kid covered up and retreated to the ropes. Barnes closed in on him but he managed to get himself out of harm's way. The two men sized each other up and suddenly The Kid rushed in and connected the Bajan with a left jab, then a straight right, that flung Barnes against the ropes. He moved in but Bisram, his eyes glued to the clock, rang the bell to end the first round.

The Kid sat on his stool and Cornerman Collins removed his mouth guard. Collins held a bottle of water to The Kid's mouth and he took a lengthy drink. Sonilal looked over at Barnes who was also having a drink. Barnes eyes locked with his and Sonilal thought he saw some respect there. Collins replaced his mouth guard and the bell sounded for the second round.

The Kid came charging out of his corner again, only this time the Bajan was ready… he sidestepped The Kid and connected with a left hook to the side of the head; The Kid was rattled. The Bajan pounced on him, but The Kid had heart, he stood up and went toe-to-toe with the Bajan; the crowd went wild. The two men were wadding into each other: left, right, left, each absorbing telling blows that would have decked lesser conditioned men, then the bell rang to end the second round and the referee separated the two.

Round Three, Four and Five saw the men more cautious. They were carefully stalking each other, looking for an opening to land the big punch.

Round Six and the action heated up: The Kid came at Barnes with a straight right but Barnes ducked out of the way and caught The Kid with a short left to the jaw; The Kid was unbalanced. Barnes moved in with a wicked left-right combination followed by a sizzling uppercut and The Kid went down hard; the crowd was silent.

One, two, three, counted the referee, and The Kid rose with the chant of his name. The referee checked his eyes and gave clearance for the fight to continue. Barnes came in for the kill but the bell sounded to end the round.

Sonilal sat on his stool and Collins took the guard out of his mouth.

'Bathe me... bathe me!' he said and Collins poured water unto his head.

Sonilal shook his head, sending water in all direction. He looked relieved.

'When you get back in there, stay away from him for a while, catch your breath, mate,' said Collins.

'Don't worry,' Sonilal hissed, 'I will break his ass.'

Mouth guard back in, the bell sounded for Round Seven:

Barnes came at The Kid, but he began moving from side-to-side, making it difficult for Barnes to cut him off. He then stuck out his face to Barnes who lunged at him with a swinging right, but The Kid jerked back and Barnes missed; the bawdy crowd disparaged the Bajan's reach. Barnes rushed The Kid and backed him into the ropes. The Kid covered up his head and Barnes went to the body with some hurtful blows. The Kid escaped and moved to the centre of the ring and began his lateral movement again, making it hard for Barnes to corner him.

Barnes was becoming a little frustrated and The Kid began talking to him:

'Come on, daddy... come and get it.'

The bell sounded to end the round.

Rounds Eight to Twelve were pretty even, both men having their moments.

Round Thirteen and The Kid came alive. He rushed Barnes as the bell sounded and caught him with a big right to the chin; the crowd hooted but the Bajan retreated to the ropes and covered up. The Kid went to work on the Bajan's body, with fearsome blows that threatened to dissect him. Then he sneaked in the perfect uppercut that caught the Bajan right on the chin; somewhere in the crowd, someone gasped.

The Bajan slumped to the ground.

Silence.

One, two, three, four, five; and the Bajan was up! The referee checked his eyes and clearance was given; Sonilal rushed in. The Bajan hugged him, but the referee separated both men as the bell rang.

'Jolly good punching, mate! Now you got to finish him off,' Collins said, as he removed The Kid's mouth guard

Round Fourteen and the two men circled each other, waiting for an opportunity. The Kid rushed in and Barnes caught him flush on the nose with a booming right. Blood trickled out The Kid's nostrils as he backpedalled and Barnes moved in for the kill, but The Kid swung a desperate, overhand left that collided with Barnes' profile, producing a swelling that immediately closed off almost half of his right eye. The bell sounded.

Collins treated Sonilal's nose and managed to stop the bleeding. Barnes' Cornerman was busy applying soft candle and Vaseline to his right eye, trying to stem the swelling. Sonilal took a long drink of water.

Mouth guards in again, the bell sounded.

The men came out cautiously; the crowd was cheering, willing The Kid to finish the Bajan. The Kid moved in with a short left jab that snapped back the Bajan's head. The Bajan countered with a fierce uppercut that almost decked The Kid. The kid covered up against the ropes, and the Bajan went to the body, pummeling The Kid with devastating blows. The Kid came off the ropes and caught the Bajan with a straight right that sent him reeling across the ring; the crowd became frenzied. The Bajan composed himself and caught The Kid with a crisp left. Both men were at it again, toe-to-toe they went, delivering and receiving wicked blows. The bell rang to end the fight but the battle raged on and the referee had to step in to separate the warriors. The crowd cheered its approval.

All three judges scored the fight a draw. The prizes were shared equally between the two men and the festivities went on late into the night.

The next day Barnes came into the shop, sporting a swollen right eye. Arthur took down a bottle of his finest and a glass and passed it to Barnes but the Bajan pushed the liquor back to him.

"I'm finished with this stuff, man. You realised what happened yesterday?"

'Well, The Kid put up a damn good fight,' Arthur admitted.

'We have unearthed a rare talent, my friend. We need to test it and see how far it could reach.'

They contacted Collins and registered Sonilal in the Island Wide Golden Gloves Amateur Boxing Competition, scheduled to begin in three months. Barnes and Collins went to work on the young warrior, Barnes passing on his years of ring savvy and experience, and Collins imparting all his technical knowledge and expertise. Together they turned the Mystery Kid into an awesome, fighting machine. Sonilal ploughed through all *comers* in the welter weight division and into the grand finals, which were to be held in the capital city of Port of Spain.

At these finals, scouts came from different parts of the world, each hoping to spot the next world champion, and when they saw Sonilal in action they were convinced. Sonilal won the welterweight crown in three, ferocious rounds of boxing. An

American scout offered him a contract immediately and he was so impressed with Sonilal's conditioning that he offered jobs to Bill Barnes and Tom Collins too but Collins, who wanted to enjoy his retirement, refused. Bill Barnes became the assistant trainer at the large gym in New York where Sonilal was based and he also acted as the cornerman for him when he fought.

Arthur and Daisy got married and fused together their many races, producing the most exotic twins one could ever see, a boy and a girl. Arthur and Daisy took over the day-to-day running of the shop, while Ping fussed over his grandchildren. The Mystery Kid was making waves in the U.S.A., having never lost a fight in the welterweight division and ranking number three in the world. Whenever The Kid fought, the whole village would gather in the shop to listen to the fight on Ping's radio. Arguments would break out between the fishermen during the fight, each and every one of them who patronised Teresa claiming to be Sonilal's father. Sometimes these arguments would turn into a fight but there was always Arthur and Daisy to keep the peace. When Sonilal won the world boxing welterweight belt on the 13th August 1962, on a hot summer night, in Madison Square Garden, he gave it to the Bajan cornerman. Bill Barnes lifted it into the air and was promptly snapped by a New York newspaper photographer.

It was a picture that should have been taken nine years earlier.

The investigation

It was Sunday 31st August 1969 and Mr. Jack was a very busy man. He was packing things into his car, but somehow he just couldn't get everything to fit: suits, boxes of groceries, books, shoes, grips filled with clothing, miscellaneous articles and of course his beloved tenor pan. He was preparing to leave for his new posting as the headmaster of the Icacos School. Mr. Jack looked at his watch: it was one-thirty in the afternoon. It was times like these that he wished his wife Lydia was here. He packed, re-packed and still couldn't find space for everything. Then he started eliminating items and these he took back to the apartment. He could always take these down when he returned the following weekend. He locked the apartment and began his journey.

Icacos was a long way from San Fernando and Mr. Jack shifted around in his seat trying to find the most comfortable spot. The car was not a new one by any means but it was faithful, already he was leaving the town of San Fernando behind. Mr. Jack was excited, rural postings were his specialties, another chance to broaden the horizon of the *steelband* movement. He already had two rural postings, Moruga and Williamsville, and both these villages had no resident steelband sides when he got there but when he left, they each had bands of over twenty playing members. Mr. Jack never fooled himself, or anyone else: the steelband movement was his first calling, head mastering was only about paying his bills. He was now on the road called Mosquito Creek, travelling southwest. A cool sea breeze wafted into the car and Mr. Jack gently depressed the x and relaxed himself; it was a pleasant drive along the lagoon, all its green mangrove trees on the left, and the smooth seas of the Gulf of Paria on the right.

He began humming one of Lord Kitchener's tunes, *Tourist Dame*, softly then his thoughts shifted to Lydia and his two daughters, who now lived in England. The girls had gone over to study, but on completion they had gotten jobs and decided to stay. He still could not decide why Lydia had made the move: maybe she was missing the girls or maybe she was just fed up of him and his pan-mongering. He chuckled because he missed her but he had to admit that it did give him more freedom to pursue his cultural goals.

It was almost five o'clock when Mr. Jack entered the little village. Shifting to a lower gear, he slowed down and began to observe his surroundings. There were coconut trees everywhere. He could not help but notice the humble dwellings of the villagers. Groups of East Indian and African children, of varying shades of brown and black and even some creamish looking ones too, were playing at intervals along the road. Mr. Jack blew his horn and waved to them and they waved back and continued their games almost immediately. Mr. Jack was sure that if they had known that he was going to be their new headmaster, they would have waved with more enthusiasm and perhaps even have a closer look at him. He came upon a sign, *drive slowly children crossing*, and after passing a huge clump of overgrowth, consisting of trees and vines, the school appeared almost out of nowhere. It consisted of three, old, weather-beaten, wooden buildings that could have clearly used a coat of paint. The largest, which was the main school building, and the smaller, which housed the infants, were on one compound, surrounded by a white wooden picket fence. There was a large mango tree on the eastern corner of the compound. The third building, which stood outside the fence but adjoined it by means of a gate, was the headmaster's house. It was a simple, two bedroom affair. Mr. Jack climbed the three steps that led to the door, took the keys out of his pocket and opened it.

The next morning Mr. Jack arose early and prepared his breakfast. He shaved, bathed, ate and put on his black suit; he always wore his black suit on a Monday morning. He took up his valise, opened the gate and stepped into the school yard where the children were already milling around and staring at Mr. Jack curiously. He entered the main school building, where the school staff were already assembled, and introduced himself. There were six of them:

Mrs. Mohammed, who taught both the first and second year infant classes; Miss. King, who taught Standard One; Miss. Jones, Standard Two; Mrs. Bristol, Standard Three; Miss Thackorie, Standard Four; and the lone gentleman, a tall neatly dressed Indian fellow named Mr. Rajnath, who taught Standard Five.

Mr. Jack himself would teach the post primary classes, Standard Six and Seven.

On the second day of school, Mr. Jack brought along his tenor pan and during the recess period, played some of the sweetest notes that the children and staff had ever heard. From that day on, Mr. Jack kept the pan in the school's cupboard and two o'clock every afternoon, he would assemble his both classes and take them out under the mango tree and there he taught the students how to beat notes on the pan.

After a few days settling in, Mr. Jack began to roam the village, questioning the villagers, whom he met, about their knowledge of the steelband movement. To his great surprise the villagers knew little or nothing, but this pleased him even more because he loved the excitement of starting from scratch. Within a week, Mr. Jack had dispatched a letter to the oil company in Point Fortin, asking for a donation of two dozen, empty steel drums to begin a steelband in the village of Icacos. Two weeks later, a reply arrived, requesting directions of the location where the pans were to be dropped off. Mr. Jack was elated. He wrote a letter thanking the company for its quick response, furnished them with the directions to the headmaster's quarters at Icacos and dispatched it immediately.

That evening, Mr. Jack went about the village, inviting everyone who was interested in learning to beat pan to a meeting the following night on the school's compound. There was a great buzz in the village and the people came out in great numbers to the meeting. Mr. Jack briefed them about the movement and told them about the empty drums that would be arriving sometime soon.

'What we need ladies and gentlemen,' he said, 'is a piece of land where we could set up a pan shed.'

A fellow by the name of Harris stepped forward and said he had a vacant piece of land, about one hundred and fifty yards down the road from the school, and he was willing to give the use of it. Mr. Jack formed a committee to oversee the building of the shed and invited anyone who wanted to donate old galvanise or lumber to drop them off at the site. In one week, a proper shed stood on the site that was donated by Mr. Harris.

The arrival of the empty drums the following Monday caused quite a stir and when Logan Brown came by taxi on Thursday, paid a ten minutes courtesy call on Mr. Jack at the school, and then walked straight to the pan shed, took out his hammer and started pounding the steel drums into shape, that was when the big buzz really started. Logan Brown was a pan tuner. Mr. Jack had Brown waiting in the wings for the arrival of the empty drums ever since he had posted the letter to the oil company. Brown lived to tune pans. He had worked together with Mr. Jack on his two previous projects, both men being friends ever since they were little boys. Brown was a paid pan tuner during the carnival season but in the off season he would work for free once you could provide him with a place to stay and some food to eat. Mr. Jack had made arrangements for Brown to stay with him in the headmaster's quarters. Brown was a quiet man who worked continuously. The whole village would turn out at the pan shed on evenings to watch him work and they especially enjoyed helping him light the big bonfires at night over which he heated his pans. When the tuning was finished, Logan Brown returned to San Fernando.

Mr. Jack began to teach the villagers to play pan music every evening after school. Sometimes he would go to the pan shed at lunch time and would not return to school until the following day. As time progressed, Mr. Jack chose seven boys from the Standard Six and Seven classes, whom he had long been tutoring on the tenor pan, and together with seventeen other villagers, who were making progress, he formed his band of twenty-four and named it: *Beach Combers Steel Orchestra*. Then it became standard procedure that Mr. Jack would leave the school every day at lunch time, marching with his seven post primary boys down to the pan shed where he would join up with the other seventeen members, and they would practice various tunes for the rest of the afternoon. On these afternoons, he would leave the school in the trusted hands of Mr. Rajnath.

Terry Rajnath came through the school's monitoring system and went on to become a full-fledged teacher; a brilliant person and many felt if he was given the chance at higher education, he would have excelled. Mr. Jack had great respect for him in fact Rajnath had once saved Mr. Jack from a very nasty situation. It happened like this:

Mr. Jack was teaching Standard Six and every time he turned his back to the class to write on the blackboard, a fellow in the back row would start making noises, like if he was beating a pan, but when Mr. Jack turned around the culprit would stop. This went on for a while and then Mr. Jack made as if he was going to write again but suddenly turned, caught the culprit and by instinct he flung a duster at the boy. Unfortunately, the wooden part of the duster caught the boy over his eye and opened a deep gash. The boy left the class and ran straight home, where he gave his father, Mohan, the story. Mohan sharpened his cutlass and went to the school with intentions of hacking Mr. Jack to pieces. When he climbed the steps and entered the building, teachers and students scampered in all directions but Mohan managed to trap Mr. Jack in a corner and as he was about to deliver, Rajnath fearlessly stepped between both men and started to talk soothingly to Mohan.

'Come on, Mr. Mohan,' he said, 'we could talk this thing over, you don't have to let it get this far. Please… give me the cutlass,' and reluctantly Mohan gave the cutlass to Rajnath. 'Thank you Mr. Mohan, now let's go over to the shop and have a drink and we will talk this over.' Then he turned to Mr. Jack and said, 'I suppose you would not mind paying for this drink.'

Quite willingly, Mr. Jack reached into his pocket and produced a five dollar note and placed it in Rajnath's hand, and he and Mohan went off to the rum shop. Mr. Jack never knew what Rajnath said to Mohan at the rumshop, but they both returned to the school after about an hour and Mohan fumbled an apology to Mr. Jack:

'Ah sorry, Sah, ah reely sorry.'

Mr. Jack and Mr. Rajnath became good friends but Rajnath had a fault and Mr. Jack knew about it too; Terry Rajnath had a drinking problem. What started off at an early age, as a simple pasttime having a drink with his friends, over the years turned into a chronic problem. Because of his easygoing ways and his status as a teacher, many sought out his company and on afternoons when he passed by the rum shop on his way home, the fishermen would call out to him and say: 'Teach, come and fire off one with the boys, man,' and Rajnath would oblige and sit there, firing off a couple drinks and having conversation with the men. Rajnath began looking forward to these afternoon sessions and as time progressed the sessions became longer. In due course, it was not an uncommon sight to see three or four fishermen, around seven o'clock in the afternoon, loading a well-dressed but drunken Rajnath into the tray of a fish truck and taking him home, he being unable to complete this task by himself. When Mr. Jack arrived at Icacos, Rajnath, at thirty six years of age, was at the peak of his drinking career.

The rumshop was about one hundred yards lower down the Icacos main road from the school. Immediately after the shop, a secondary road ran across the main road thereby creating a *four road junction*. To get to the pan shed from the school you had to pass the rum shop, swing right at the junction and walk down a further fifty yards. So when Mr. Jack left the school in the charge of Mr. Rajnath on afternoons to go to his pan sessions, Rajnath would be looking at Mr. Jack through the school's window and as Mr. Jack and his seven students rounded the corner and went out of sight, Rajnath would make a mad dash for the rumshop and have a couple drinks and according to how the spirits moved him, he might even spend the remainder of the afternoon partaking thereof.

At times like these Miss Thackorie, the Standard Four teacher, would go over to Mr. Rajnath's class, giving his students work to do and trying to maintain general discipline. Jennifer Thackorie had been transferred from the Cedros School to the Icacos School about one year before. Only twenty-two years of age, she was deeply infatuated with Mr. Rajnath, a fact that was concealed even from Mr. Rajnath and known only unto herself. She was attracted to his good looks and cool demeanor, but more so, she saw Mr. Rajnath as a man who needed someone to take care of him and she fancied herself as being the right person for the job. She was not the first one either. Many a female teacher, who had passed through the Icacos School system, was at one-point-in-time-or-another infatuated with Mr. Rajnath but they always found out that the love of Rajnath's life walked not on two feet but lay in the bottles on the shelves of the village rumshop.

Around this time, a concerned villager began writing letters to the Ministry of Education, complaining about the extracurricular activities of Mr. Jack and Mr. Rajnath that was *actually* taking place during school hours. As protocol demanded at this time, a letter had to be sent from the ministry to the school informing them of the date when the supervisor would be visiting and when Mr. Jack received the letter he had ample time to put his house in order. When the supervisor, Mr. Gordon, arrived the school was a model of discipline and learning. He was impressed and took back a very favourable report of the staff and students of the Icacos School. The letters were then seen merely as someone who was trying to create mischief. But the letters kept coming to the desk of School Supervisor Three, Miss Michelle Duncan, who was in charge of the primary schools supervisory division. Miss Duncan was a very shrewd person and she recognised the persistence of the letter writer; perhaps there was something here that they were overlooking. She sent for Mr. Gordon and when he arrived she said to him:

'Mr. Gordon, we keep getting these letters from Icacos and I'm wondering if maybe there is something we might be missing.'

Mr. Gordon folded his arms. 'Well, what do you suggest?' he asked.

'I would like to send you down there on a mission,' she said.

Mr. Gordon smiled. 'KGB stuff, Miss Duncan?'

She smiled. 'Yes, Mr. Gordon, KGB stuff.'

Mr. Gordon removed his glasses, took a piece of cloth out of his pocket and began wiping the lens. 'And how are we going to proceed?'

'Well firstly,' she said, 'I will not want you to use your own car. Use mine; it will give you that little element of surprise.'

It was one-thirty, Friday afternoon, and the Icacos School was in disarray. Three teachers had taken time off to go for salaries. Miss Jones had left at lunch time because she had gotten a message that her mother was ill and Mr. Jack and Mr. Rajnath were out on their usual afternoon pursuits. Miss Thackorie, the lone teacher present, had long given up trying to maintain discipline in the school. She sat on a chair, with her head resting on a table, and shut out the world. Unsupervised, the children were making use of their good luck. A Standard Three student was marking obscene words on the blackboard; Standard Four children were pitching marbles in the walkway; Standard Six students had a pack of cards and were playing *All Fours* and some children were making jets out of copybook pages and flying them in the school's airspace while others screamed and chased the paper planes.

Mr. Gordon was approaching his destination. The drive was long but easy, thanks to the black, heavily-tinted Super Saloon with its air-conditioning system and stereo music. He slowed down and his thoughts went back to the *mission* and he hoped to God that he would not find anything to implicate anyone. He turned off the music, drove quietly into the school yard, switched off the motor and opened his door. Mr. Gordon could not believe his ears! The noise that was coming out of the Icacos School could have been more easily associated with that of a fish market. He climbed the three steps and entered the school; one of the paper jets that were encircling the air space suddenly dipped and lodged between Mr. Gordon's spectacles, missing his left eye by a millimeter. Mr. Gordon was enraged.

'Silence!' he boomed.

The transformation was immediate. Miss Thackorie jumped to her feet, knocking over the table in the process.

'Miss Thackorie, what is going on here?' he demanded.

Miss Thackorie began to cry.

'Miss Thackorie, where is Mr. Jack and Mr. Rajnath?'

Miss Thackorie wiped her eyes with the back of her hands.

'I don't know, Sir,' she replied.

Mr. Gordon turned to the students. 'Does anyone here know where I can find Mr. Jack and Mr. Rajnath?'

A little fellow got up from his seat.

'Yes, young man?' asked Mr. Gordon.

'Sir, Mr. Jack out by the pan shed teaching pan and Mr. Rajnath? Mr. Rajnath by the rumshop drinking rum.'

Mr. Gordon scratched his chin. 'Can you take me to these two places?' he asked.

'Yes Sir,' said the little boy and he followed Mr. Gordon to the car and sat in the passenger's seat. Mr. Gordon reversed the black car out of the gate and then continued slowly along the Icacos main road.

'That is the shop there, Sir, right on the corner like I tell you,' said the little boy.

Mr. Gordon drove up to the rumshop, stopped and came out. The jukebox was belting out the hit tune of the day, *My boy lollipop*, and there was Mr. Rajnath, lying on the floor of the rumshop, immaculately dressed in his white, long-sleeve shirt and grey pants, completely drunk. Mr. Gordon hurried back into the car.

'Now, where is that pan shed?' he asked.

'You have to take a right here now, Sir, and it just a little bit down the road.'

Mr. Jack and the Beach Combers Steel Orchestra had just finished beating a perfect rendition of the Mighty Sparrow's *Mae Mae* and the members were all celebrating. Mr. Jack could not believe that they had attained such perfection in such a short time frame. A member of the band was drinking a beer and passed it to Mr. Jack, who had never drank alcohol in his life, and the headmaster was so elated with the performance that he raised the bottle to his lips, said cheers, and took a little sip of the contents. The black, heavily-tinted Super Saloon was passing by slowly at the same time and Mr. Gordon caught Mr. Jack in the very act.

'My goodness!' he exclaimed and shook his head. He kept on driving until he found a turning spot, then he dropped the little boy off at the school and sped off to Port of Spain.

When the little boy returned to the school, Miss Thackorie questioned him:

'What did Mr. Gordon see?'

The little boy placed his two hands in his pockets and said:

'He see Mr. Rajnath drunk on the floor of the rumshop and Mr. Jack drinking beer by the pan shed.'

'And what did he say?' asked Miss Thackorie.

'He say "My goodness!" and he shake he head, Miss.'

Miss Thackorie went to the school's cupboard, opened the door and took out a guava whip that was stored there. She concealed it behind her back and beckoned the little boy to come to her. The little fellow approached her cautiously and when he was within reach, she grabbed him and gave him a sound licking with the whip. Then she began to cry.

Monday morning, Miss Thackorie gave all the details to Mr. Jack and Mr. Rajnath. Mr. Jack was quite worried to say the least. At lunchtime, the two gentlemen remained in school and discussed the problem at length.

'You know what will happen now, Raj?' asked Mr. Jack.

Rajnath shrugged his shoulders.

'I'll tell you,' said Mr. Jack. 'Mr. Gordon would submit a report today on the desk of School Supervisor Three. She would read it and arrange a high-powered team and they will be down here within the week to grill our asses.'

Mr. Rajnath stood there cool and composed. Mr. Jack could not believe the man.

Miss Michelle Duncan had just finished reading the report and sent for Mr. Gordon.

'Pretty serious stuff,' she said, placing the report on the desk.

'Yep! Pretty serious stuff!' said Mr. Gordon.

Miss Duncan called in a clerk and asked her to get the files of a Mr. Armis Jack and a Mr. Terry Rajnath of the Icacos School. The clerk brought in the files and Miss Duncan went through them carefully.

'Nothing in here to suggest such a breakdown,' she said. 'It describes Mr. Rajnath as a model teacher and hard worker who came through the monitoring system and Mr. Jack as a very inspirational and motivated headmaster.' She passed the files to Mr. Gordon who browsed through them. 'We'll have to go down there and sort this out,' she concluded.

'Definitely,' said Mr. Gordon.

'I'm thinking of a team of three. I myself would sit in on this one, you of course and I will ask School Supervisor Two Mrs. Bartlet to accompany us.'

Mr. Gordon fumbled with his tie. 'When do we leave?'

'I'm thinking of Thursday,' she said.

The ensuing days were tense ones for Mr. Jack. He was visibly worried and limited his visits to the pan shed to after school sessions only. Mr. Rajnath, cool as ever, was still hitting off a few drinks but he was doing so a lot more discretely. Thursday morning, during the recess break, Mr. Jack spoke to Rajnath:

'Raj, it could be any day now, man. I'm worried sick.'

'You worry too much, old fellow,' said Rajnath.

'Easy for you to say,' replied Mr. Jack.

'Well… you told me it was the first time you had tasted a beer,' said Mr. Rajnath.

'And that's the truth,' Mr. Jack reconfirmed for the thousandth time.

'Well, you don't have to worry that much, they always go easier on first time offenders. Anyway I'm going over to the shop for a minute,' said Rajnath.

'Raj, my good friend, I beseech you not to touch that stuff,' he said.

'Don't worry, Mr. Jack, I'm just going over to pay a bill.'

Rajnath hustled over to the rumshop and called for a drink and four mints. He poured the drink down his throat, peeled the paper off one of the mints, popped the mint into his mouth and hurried back to the school. Mr. Jack was waiting. He tried to get as close as possible to Mr. Rajnath, to see if he could smell any alcohol, but Rajnath's mint had worked perfectly. Mr. Jack managed a smile then he slipped back into worrying.

'You know Raj, all my long years of service could go down the drain with this matter,' he said.

'Listen, my friend, you just have to speak from the heart. You are a cultural person, pushing something that you believe in. They will understand.'

Mr. Jack gained solace in his friend's words. 'But Raj? How come I never see you around the pan shed? I can't even ask you what you think of our music.'

'I've heard your music,' said Rajnath.

'And how is that so?' inquired Mr. Jack.

'I hear you all the time from the rumshop,' he said.

'You mean you were going to the rumshop every evening when I left you in charge?' asked Mr. Jack.

'Well, most evenings anyway,' said Rajnath.

Mr. Jack looked disappointed then he said:

'Seriously… what do you think of our music then?'

Rajnath looked him in the face, scratched the back of his own head, smiled and said:

'Groovy melodies, Mr. Jack… groovy melodies.'

The high powered team in the black Super Saloon was almost at their destination. Mr. Gordon was driving the car; Mrs. Bartlet was in the front passenger's seat and Miss Duncan, who was in charge of the team, sat in the back. Miss Michelle Duncan was a beautiful, black woman and at thirty-five years of age she was senior to Mrs. Bartlet and Mr. Gordon who were both much older than her. This was not because she was beautiful, but because she was brilliant. She had done well at school and then went on to university and had gotten her degree in education. She lived with her father, her mother being deceased. Her father, Mr. Aubrey Duncan, was a retired attorney and was responsible for guiding her through her education. Miss Duncan was a career-minded person, a problem solver and moreover her solutions were always practical and very humane. She was loved and respected by her peers.

It was five-minutes-past-eleven when the black car eased its way into the school yard.

The three occupants came out and after strained formalities, Mr. Jack was instructed to evacuate the infants' building and move the children to the bigger school building. Mr. Jack knew right away that they were going to use the small building to conduct their investigation. His heart sank. They arranged a big table with three chairs on one side and one chair on the other. Everyone except the three supervisors left the building. After consulting for about five minutes, they called in Mr. Jack and made him close the door after he entered. Before they could begin to question him, Mr. Jack remembered the words that Mr. Rajnath told him earlier and asked if he could say something. They agreed and Mr. Jack began telling them of his passionate love for pan, his involvement in the steelband movement and his achievements in his two previous rural postings – Miss Duncan's eyes brightened as the story went on. Then he told them about his arrival at Icacos, teaching the post primary students to beat the tenor pan, the arrival of the empty drums, the forming of the band, up until when Mr. Gordon saw him with the beer in his hand and then he stopped.

Miss Duncan smiled. She opened her briefcase, sifted through a bit and came out with an envelope. She said:

'I got this correspondence one week ago.'

She opened the envelope, took out a letter and passed it to Mrs. Bartlet who read it and passed it to Mr. Gordon. The letter went like this:

Dear Miss Duncan,

Seeing that the steelpan is such a treasure to our national heritage, we would like to incorporate it into our school system. Please identify someone whom we can use as a coordinator to oversee such a project.

Yours respectfully,
Sylvia Carrington
Minister of Education

When Mr. Gordon finished reading the letter, he passed it back to Miss Duncan who put it back into its envelope and returned it to her briefcase. She then turned to Mr. Jack. She said:

'I understand that your pan shed is not very far from here. Could you rounds up some of your members and bring your pans into the schoolyard and play something for us?'

'Why, I'll be delighted to, Miss Duncan.'

And Mr. Jack got his post primary boys and sent them out in all different directions to find the members of the band. Then, he went to his friend Harris, who had an old Bedford truck, and Harris brought the pans to the school for him. In quick time the boys had found thirteen members of the band and together with the seven post primary boys, Mr. Jack had a solid band of twenty, playing members and all his pans assembled in the school yard. By this time the villagers sensed that something was happening and they lined up around the picket fence of the school, then the school children came out and lined up in front of the school and so it was that Mr. Jack and the *Beach Combers Steel Orchestra* had a lovely audience and they did not disappoint. Pan melodies, as never heard before, were coaxed from those old drums by the gentle playing sticks of the members of the band. Everyone began dancing around and even the supervisors stood up and began clapping in time with the music. Miss Duncan was elated. When the session was completed, Mr. Gordon turned to Miss Duncan.

'Well, Miss Michelle, I guess you have found your coordinator.'

'Yes, I think we have found the right man for the job.'

She took the envelope out of her briefcase, took the letter out of it and walked over to Mr. Jack. She gave him the letter and he began to read. When he was finished she asked:

'Would you be interested in filling such a vacancy?'

Mr. Jack was elated. 'I'll be greatly honored to do so, Miss Duncan.'

The three supervisors then returned to the infants' building and it was the turn of Mr. Rajnath to be interviewed. He closed the door behind him and was told to sit on the vacant chair. Mr. Rajnath sat down on the chair and folded his arms in a childlike manner. Miss Duncan reached slowly into her briefcase, took out his files and placed them on the table.

'Mr. Rajnath,' she said, 'I've studied your files on more than one occasion and there is nothing in there to suggest the sort of behavior that you have been exhibiting of late. You came through the monitoring system, brilliant teacher, hard worker… where did things go wrong?'

'I'm sorry, Miss Duncan. I'm truly sorry.'

'We know that you are sorry, Mr. Rajnath, but in order for us to help you we must know what drove you to this. Is there some problem or some situation that triggered it off?'

Miss Duncan had played right into the hands of Mr. Rajnath and he was not going to let her off. He looked into her eyes and with a sad face said softly:

'I guess so.'

'Well come on, Mr. Rajnath, tell us about it,' Mrs. Bartlet coaxed.

'Okay,' said Mr. Rajnath, unfolding his arms and resting them on the table. 'I grew up right next door to a little boy whose name was Toby. As far back as my memory could go it seems Toby was there. My first-day-at-school-fears were greatly alleviated because my friend, Toby, was there and while the other children were crying for their parents, Toby and I were playing games and having fun. We grew up like brothers but when he was twenty-two years old tragedy struck.'

Rajnath paused and seemed reluctant to continue.

'Well go on, Mr. Rajnath,' urged Miss Duncan.

Rajnath removed his hands from the table and folded them again.

'Toby's both parents were killed in a car crash. From that day on, Toby was not the same. He became very distant and started avoiding people. Whenever I tried to engage him in conversation he would duck out of it quickly and go his way. The years went by and Toby began acting strangely. One day I was coming from Point Fortin in a taxi and, closer to the village of Fullerton, I saw Toby walking with a huge stone upon his head in the middle of the road. The car almost ran him over! The driver stopped, I got out and the driver came out too. Toby put the stone on the ground... on top of the stone was a sardine pan with a dead frog in it. Toby started to curse loudly:

"What the f- does wrong with allyuh drivers? You don't see I doing a state funeral, man? You bypass all my outriders and police escort and almost run over the chief pallbearer and the deceased. I have a good mind to take your blasted license."

He picked back up the stone with the sardine pan and the dead frog and placed it back on his head and then he turned to me and asked:

"You have cigarettes Raj?"

I said yes.

He said, "Light one and put it in my mouth for me."

I lit the cigarette and placed it in his mouth. He blew out a puff of smoke and muttered under his breath:

"F-ing, delinquent drivers, don't even have respect for a state funeral."

And he began walking again. Toby was barefooted and it was then I realised that the soles of his feet were festered and bloody. Leaving him was impossible. I paid the driver his fare and told him to go ahead and I began walking with Toby. I said:

"Toby, who funeral you carrying there, boy?"

He spat out the cigarette butt and said:

"The Minister of National Security.'

"Oh shucks, boy, only this morning I hearing about this funeral on the radio. They postpone the funeral to tomorrow, because the Prime Minister of Guyana's flight get delayed and the two of them was real buddies."

He turned to me and asked:

"You hear that on the radio in truth?"

"Positive," I said.

"But what the arse I will do with this body now?" he asked.

"Just lay it in state, man," I said.

"In this wilderness?"

I said:

"Look. Right under that coconut tree there is a good spot. Come I will help you put him down."

He said: "That look like a nice peaceful place in truth," and we went off the road and carefully took down the stone with the deceased and placed it under the coconut tree. Then we went back onto the road and stopped the next taxi that was heading to Icacos and I managed to coax him in. The next day, it would seem, Toby resumed his pall bearing, because I met the taxi driver of the day before and he told me that he passed Toby on the Cedros main road with the said stone on his head around ten o'clock that morning. From that time on Toby would disappear from the village for days and suddenly he would pop up again.

One day, a fire started in a wooden house in the village. There were three children trapped in the building. Their mother had gone to the shop to purchase some items and had left them home alone. By the time the alarm was raised, the fire was out of control and the children were bawling inside. Because of the intense heat, no one ventured near the building, but then came Toby. He broke down the door, ran into the house and brought out the three children safely. Then the smallest of the children, a little girl held on to his hand and said:

"Uncle Toby, I forget my dolly in the house."

Uncle Toby did not hesitate. He ran back into the building and within two minutes he threw the dolly through a window. Everyone was bawling: "Come out Toby! Come out Toby!" but Toby was never to exit that building alive again. He never screamed, never made a noise, he just remained in there and burned. When the fire brigade arrived, all that was remaining of him fitted into a small plastic bag. When I got the news I was devastated. I felt guilty. I knew I had not done enough for my friend and that was when I turned to the bottle for solace.'

Tears were running down the cheeks of Miss Duncan and Mrs. Bartlet and even Mr. Gordon managed a sniffle or two.

'You poor man,' said Miss Duncan and she walked around the table and placed her arm around Mr. Rajnath and comforted him.

Then she sat down with her comrades and they began consulting, while Mr. Rajnath stared sheepishly around the room. The consultation lasted about fifteen minutes and when they were finished Miss Duncan said:

'Mr. Rajnath, we will allow you to remain teaching as per normal, however we would ask you to practice restraint in your extracurricular activities. You are shaping the minds of our future generations and you know how impressionable they are at this age. In addition, we will be enrolling you in Alcoholics Anonymous at the Couva Community Centre. We will send you a correspondence by post, informing you of the starting date and the duration of the course.'

That night, over dinner, Miss. Duncan gave full details of the days happening to her Father. Mr. Duncan was amazed at her stories.

'Quite an intriguing day,' he said.

'I dare say. Imagine meeting two extraordinary gentlemen in one day!'

'Well the ends served the means. I think Mr. Jack fits that new job perfectly and I hope… what's the other guy's name?'

'Mr. Rajnath.'

'I do hope that Mr. Rajnath is able to lick his habit.'

'Well, I certainly hope so! He seems like such a nice person.'

Twelve days later, Mr. Rajnath received his correspondence. The course was to begin the coming Saturday, from nine-thirty in the morning to one-thirty in the afternoon, and would continue every week, for a duration of three months. Mr. Jack's last day in charge of the Icacos School was the Friday before Mr. Rajnath was due to begin his course. Icacos gave him a grand send off, with the *Beach Combers Steel Orchestra* playing their full repertoire of songs in his honor. Mr. Jack made a very emotional speech at the end of the performance and, with tears in his eyes, bade farewell to Mr. Rajnath and the staff of the school and left to take up his new appointment with the ministry.

Saturday morning Mr. Rajnath awoke at five and by six o'clock he was already in a taxi making his way to Couva. Since the investigation, he had not taken a drink of alcohol and was actually making a serious attempt at rehabilitating himself. When he got there, he sat through the testimonies, listening attentively, and at the end of the session was surprised by Miss Duncan's appearance at the centre.

'Hello Mr. Rajnath, it's very nice to see that you have kept your appointment,' she said.

'Why, hello Miss Duncan, nice of you to be checking up on me too.'

'Duty bound, Mr. Rajnath, duty bound,' she smiled.

Every Saturday, Mr. Rajnath religiously made his trip to Couva and duty-bound Miss Duncan found the time to check up on him. She would arrive a few minutes before the end of the classes and wait for them to finish and she would sit and engage Mr. Rajnath in conversation. Mr. Rajnath was a good listener and an easy talker, humorous to boot and the conversations began to get lengthy. By the fifth Saturday, Mr. Duncan, observant man that he was, noticed that his daughter was taking much longer to ready herself on a Saturday morning. She was always a classy dresser, but she dressed quickly; now she was taking her time, almost fussing over herself.

It was Friday night and sleep was eluding Mr. Rajnath. Tomorrow would be his seventh journey to Couva and his conscience was giving him a hard time. He was doing great in the classes, in fact, alcohol was a thing of the past, but the lie he had told to Miss Duncan during the investigation was sitting heavy on his chest. Miss Duncan was such a nice person; she had shown him respect, kindness and encouragement. It was not the lie itself that bothered him but the manner in which he had told it. He could remember that he thoroughly enjoyed himself during its dispensation and now he was reaping the whirlwind for his careless imagination. He made up his mind... tomorrow he would do the right thing.

That Saturday, Michelle Duncan returned home a little earlier than normal. Mr. Duncan was reading the newspaper. He looked at his watch.

'Home early my dear.'

'Yes, a bit early,' she said.

She looked tense and began pacing the floor. Mr. Duncan looked at her from behind his newspaper and asked:

'Is something the matter, Miche?'

'You bet.'

'Something you want to talk about?'

'Remember that episode Mr. Rajnath told about his friend Toby?'

'Why, of course, who could forget a story like that?'

'It was a lie!'

'You're joking,' he said incredulously.

'I wish I were. The nerve of that guy, I can't believe there are people like him walking around.'

'And how do you know it was a lie?' he asked.

'He told me so himself,' she answered.

'Now that makes quite a difference, dear. It takes a lot of courage for someone to admit that they had lied.'

'I'm never going back to that centre to check on him again, dad.' And she continued pacing the floor.

Mr. Duncan pretended to be reading his newspaper but was observing his daughter. Normally a very calm person, she was restless, almost agitated and every now and then she would mutter:

'Jeez! I can't believe this guy.'

Mr. Duncan was clearly amused because he had never seen his daughter worked up like this before. He had waited long years just for this moment. Finally, someone had gotten to her. There had been suitors coming around over the years but always career-minded, she never seemed interested in any of them. Clearly this fellow had caught her off balance. Mr. Duncan was looking at her, almost as someone watched a movie and he was thoroughly enjoying himself. She stopped pacing and stood in front of him and said sharply:

'Remember this, dad: I'm never going to Couva to check on that guy again.'

'Okay my dear. But in all seriousness, remember that it would've taken a lot of soul searching and humility for him to admit to you, like he did.'

The next Saturday Michelle paced the floor while Mr. Duncan prepared breakfast.

'Dad, do you think I have an obligation to make sure that Mr. Rajnath attends his session?'

'Why certainly, dear, I think you have a moral obligation,' Mr. Duncan baited her.

Later on that morning, it was an amused father who opened the gate for a well-dressed, duty-bound daughter. She went that Saturday and every Saturday until the course was finished.

Six months later, Miss Michelle Duncan and Mr. Terry Rajnath were married in a wonderful ceremony. Music for the sticking of the cake was supplied by the *Belmont Boys' School Steel Orchestra*, led by the evergreen Mr. Armis Jack.

The ham bone

It have a time a piece of hardship hit Icacos that have everybody living next door to starvation. Fish not catching at all and rain not falling so nothing growing either. This situation started to develop in February and everybody hoping that things will get better. March, April, May, June and situation deteriorating; no rain, no fish. Fishermen, who came down there to make a living, start to re-migrate, some back to Moruga, some to Las Cuevas, others gone to Port of Spain and San Fernando to look for work, but the diehard Icacos fishermen not moving. Why? Because these fellars is direct descendants to St. Peter and they full of hope and faith. Well, June, July, August, things looking bad, fishermen start to get boney like Don Quixote horse. September and one of the fishermen little son learn to count in school. He so excited, he checking everything in sight. When he come home, he meet he father bareback in the gallery and he say:

"Daddy, let me check you ribs, boy."

The man so boney the child check twenty-six ribs.

October, November, December, things can't get worse; three square meals were replaced by three round ones in the form of dried coconuts because that was all the fishermen getting to eat. When a fellar passing by a house and he smell food cooking, he loitering in front the people house, hoping for an invite and sometimes he will get it, because Icacos people is nice people. Christmas approaching, everybody in the village worried, but none as much as a fellow name Joe Crepe.

Everybody in Icacos have *soodonim*, is a favourite pass time as people like to play godfather for other people children. Parents give they children nice, respectable names like John, Michael and James, and they end up getting nickname like *Cat Bake*, *Goat Stones* and *Lal Totie*. Well, Joe Crepe nickname was *Santa Clause* because the man love Christmas too bad. Joe uses to save up his money all year round just to buy all kind of nice things for Christmas and as Christmas done he start saving again for the next Christmas. This year Joe can't even put food on the table. Day after day he going out to sea in his boat but nothing catching. It seems like all the fish migrate to the north pole to spend Christmas with the real Santa. Two days before Christmas, Joe get up six o'clock in the morning, a broken man, and as he coming out the bedroom his wife, Venora, say:

"Joe, I just want you to know that if you can't buy ham this Christmas I going by my parents and stay."

Now Joe know that that is not an idle threat because the wife love ham too bad. Joe praying for a miracle and he thinking, then suddenly: the cow, man! He would sell the blasted cow. The damn thing didn't give much milk anyway. Just then a fellow run through the village bawling:

"To the beach! To the beach! Fish raise! Fish raise!"

Joe see fellars running from all directions towards the beach and he start to run too because he know that that cry meant the arrival of fish in the waters off the village. When he get down there, he could see a school of fish beating the seawater into a white foam, not too far from the shore. There was a seine boat on the beach and the men were pushing it into the water. Joe joined them. When the boat was floating, they passed the end rope of the seine to a few fellars on the beach, started the engine, made a semicircle around the school of fish with the seine and brought the attached rope to the other end of the beach. The men then split up into two groups and began pulling the seine to shore. Thousands of pounds of fish were snared in the net and when it was sold to the vendor, and the money divided, Joe had a king's ransom of two hundred and seventy-five dollars in his pocket.

Joe want to surprise Venora, so he ain't tell she a thing. He bathe, change his clothes and hop a taxi for Point Fortin. As he drop off, he gone straight into a grocery store and the first thing he pick up was a nice, juicy ham. Apple, grapes, biscuit, bottle of rum, wine and all kinda nice thing, Joe full up his trolley with because in them days things rel cheap. When Joe done pay the bill he still have a nice raise in his pocket so he run over by the hardware store and he buy sandpaper, varnish, white paint and a gallon of bright orange for the gallery. Then he got a taxi, loaded his boxes into the trunk and headed back home. When he got there he placed the boxes in the kitchen and when Venora open the first one she ask:

"Joe… whey you get all these nice things, boy?" When she opened the second one and she see the ham, she start to giggle, like a little child when somebody tickling them. She say: "Joe, you really love me, boy."

Joe, smiling from ear-to-ear, start to pullout chair and table and drag them into the gallery and he start to whistle sandpaper on their edges. When he have them smooth, he start to varnish from a side. In no time at all, old thing start to look like new.

Christmas Eve morning, Joe get up five o'clock and start to rake the yard. Then he take out his gallon of white paint and start to paint the base of all the trees in his yard. In no time at all he have everything looking spic and span. He run across by the cow and give it grass and water. Then he take out the gallon of bright orange and start to paint the gallery and by evening the place looking like Christmas. When night come, Joe bathe and gone in the house to help Venora hang up the curtains. She done bake all the bread and cakes already and now she baking the ham. Joe watching Venora in all she fatness, gliding about the kitchen like a young model. Every now and then, she opening the oven door and basing the ham: a little tomato ketchup here, a little pepper sauce there and some clove and mustard, and then licking her fingers and making a pleasing sound. Joe enjoying the smell of the fresh paint and things baking, and the Christmas spirit start crawling through his veins. Joe start to hear a noise coming from further up the road and he looked at the clock; it said eight o'clock.

"What! The boys start to parang early this year! They does normally begin around half-nine," Joe said to Venora, who did not answer.

What Joe forget was that whole year the boys was starving and all of them were not lucky to be in the catch of the day before therefore a early start was vital to get a little something under the belt. So when they gone in by *Cat Bake* and they singing:

"Bring out the bread, bring out the ham, bring out the turkey, bring out the lamb… is Christmas!" they stressing on the words and they dead serious.

Only problem is *Cat Bake* was not one of the lucky ones in the big catch and all he could ah put on the table was a little rum and some biscuit and cheese. So as they drink out the little rum and clearway the biscuit and cheese, they start to make sign to one another that it was time to leave, and *Cat Bake* was glad too because he did not have anything else to offer but he join up with them hoping to find some worthy victuals also.

This time so, Joe tracking the noise and he know that the boys move from by *Cat Bake* and they over by *Ramsing*. He know that he will be next on the list, so he start to prepare the table for the boys. Rum here, coconut water there, bread, cheese, cake, apple, grapes, biscuit, but Joe done know that ham is the one thing that not reaching on that table. He himself would be grudgingly rationed a piece or two during the season, other than that Venora not sharing that ham with anyone. When ham finish baking, Venora take it out of the oven and put it on the table and as she was about to cut off a piece and taste it, she hear the boys coming up the front step. Hurriedly, she placed the ham back in the oven and closed the door. She opened the door to her bedroom and retired inside.

This time, the boys inside and Joe greeting them all around, sharing out drinking glasses as he went. Then he proposed a quick toast to friendship and love, and with that! Man! The boys start to *beat* rum and attack the goodies on the table with full force. Meanwhile, the smell of the ham was lingering in the air and *Lal Totie* take a deep breath and he say:

"Yes Joe! That ham smelling good boy!"

Then all the boys start sniffing the air like hunting dogs and they chorused:

"Yes Joe, that ham really smelling good."

Then Ramdial pleaded:

"Joe… come nah, boy! Give we a lil taste in the ham."

Joe start to panic because Ramdial is he real partner and he don't know how to refuse him, so he tiptoe and gone in the kitchen and easy like a mouse open the oven and take out the ham and place it on the table. Then he take a knife and start to cut out some thin, thin, see-through strips and pass it to the boys. Same time, Joe get urge to pee and he leave the ham on the table and run outside and lean up against a coconut tree and start to make pee. All this time, *Goat Stones*, who head bad, pick up the hot ham in his two hands and take one, big bite and pass it to the fellar next to him. The fellar put a big bite on it too and pass it to the next man and the ham start to go in a circle, disappearing as it went.

Meanwhile Venora, like she getting a premonition, put her ears close to the wall and listening. She hearing a funny sound, like when hyenas stripping a carcass. She start to cold sweat and she rush outside in time to see *Cat Bake* biting off the last piece of flesh from the ham bone. This time Joe now coming through the door from making his pee.

"Joe, you nasty bitch you! You allow these vultures to eat my ham!"

She snatch the ham bone from *Cat Bake* and start to beat Joe all over his head with it. Well the boys love Joe but they not about to interfere in husband and wife business, so they walk out the house singing:

"I saw mum-my hitting San-ta Clause."

Sharkey's run

It was eight-fifteen in the morning and the Ocean Missile had just pulled alongside Platform C in the southwest field. Captain Sharkey gave the order to the engineer to cut the engines. He used his right forefinger and flicked the sweat off his brows.

"Too darn early to be sweating like this, Carlton," he said to the engineer.

Carlton went to the engine room, switched off the engines and returned to the pilot house.

"Have a look at that sea, Carlton. Too darn calm for my liking. Something is brewing somewhere," said the captain.

Carlton looked out the window; the sea was like a sheet of glass, not a ripple.

Trident Base Terminal Foreman Tanner looked at his watch and breathed a sigh of relief. The clock said eight-twenty. He was on the go since seven, answering radios, dispatching boats, organising cargoes to be loaded and checking manifests. It was his first chance to take stock of himself. He hadn't had his breakfast as yet.

"I am going over to the canteen to get a coffee," he said to the duty dispatcher and he stepped out and made his way to the canteen.

He returned balancing two cups of coffee and slipped one towards the dispatcher. He reached into his bag, retrieved a sandwich and peeled off the foil but as he was about to sink his teeth into it, the radio activated:

"Trident Base, Trident Base, come in to the MET Office."

Tanner looked at the dispatcher, frowned, picked up the transmitter and depressed the button:

"Trident Base receiving. Over."

"Trident Base, there is an unusual weather formation developing off the east coast of Trinidad and moving in a westerly direction. Should be hitting the Gulf of Paria in three hours. Suggest that you evacuate all platforms immediately. How copy? Over."

Tanner swore inaudibly and failed to notice that his hunger had vanished. He depressed the button again:

"Message received and understood. Will commence evacuation immediately."

"Ocean Missile, Ocean Missile, come in to the Trident Base. Over."

Sharkey picked up the transmitter, depressed the button and replied:

"Ocean Missile receiving you; over."

"Ocean Missile, unusual weather system headed for the Gulf of Paria. Evacuate all three platforms in the southwest field. Over."

"Ocean Missile proceeding to commence evacuation. Over."

Carlton looked at Sharkey, looked through the window at the calm sea and shook his head:

"An old sea dog always smells a bad pot of porridge."

Tanner, back at Trident Base, proceeded to call the other nine boats in the Trident operations and ordered total evacuation of the other platforms in the Trident fields.

Carlton restarted the engines and Sharkey blew his horn. The seven men from Platform C hustled down immediately. The sailor threw off the ropes and Sharkey sleekly manipulated his controls, edging the Missile off the platform. Then he spun her around and headed towards Platform B. The Ocean Missile, fifty-two feet long and fitted with two GM 871s which equipped her with elegant speed and power, was the crown jewel of the Trident fleet. She was so agile that they called her the Cutting Horse, and the old fox Sharkey was the cowboy who coaxed the best out of her. Sharkey eased her alongside Platform B and blew his horn. Thirteen men hurried down with bags, some strapping on life jackets as they came. Sharkey backed away from the platform and headed towards Platform A. The men were already waiting on the landing and Sharkey took her alongside; eleven in all.

"Trident Base, Trident Base. Come in to the Ocean Missile."

"Trident Base receiving. Over."

"Platforms A, B and C cleared. A full complement of thirty-one passengers on board and heading to base. Over."

"Okay, Captain Sharkey, have a safe trip up. Over."

The sea was dead calm as Sharkey navigated off the platform and gracefully spun her about, and then gradually he pushed the throttles until he had her at full speed. Her bow was up and she ran with a sort of elegance that bordered arrogance. Captain Sharkey referred to her as the Old Tub or the Old Lady. Deep down inside he prided himself by her, was in love with her, like a man loves a woman and would feel every little scratch and dent he put on her and at the earliest opportunity would clean her wounds and cover it with paint. Vessel after vessel they left in their wake and Sharkey looked back at them and the faintest of smiles played on his face.

"Not bad for an old tub eh Carlton?"

Carlton took that as a compliment and smiled a toothless smile.

They were nearing the mouth of the Trident Base and Sharkey began to ease back his throttles. They entered the channel and he brought her to idle speed, then with steady hands he put her into the passenger pen. When all was secured, Sharkey and his crew made their way over to the canteen.

"Coffee all around please," said Sharkey to the attendant.

The last of the Trident fleet was now inside the base and the dispatcher was tallying his arrivals with the morning departures when, suddenly, the radio activated:

"Trident Base, Trident Base come in to Platform D. Over."

Tanner picked up the transmitter. "Trident Base receiving. Man on Platform D, what in the heavens are you still doing out there? Over."

"Requesting three bags of cansorb to finish cleaning tank on block station of Platform D. Over."

"Don't you know about the approaching storm and the evacuation? Over."

"Negative, Sir. We were inside the tank cleaning. Over."

"How many men are with you? Over."

"Two and myself. Over."

"Okay! Seek shelter in safest area of platform. Will be sending vessel to pick you up. Over." Tanner swore and looked over at the dispatcher who had finished his calculation.

The subordinate nodded. "A deficit of three, Sir."

The Duty Supervisor, hearing the conversation on the radio, came into Tanner's office.

"Three men left back on Platform D, Tanner?" he frowned.

"Yes, *Super*. According to the last report from the MET office we have one hour and a half before the shit hits the fan. Just enough time to send in a vessel. Whom do you recommend we send?"

"Send Crevelle. He's young, smart, has a good navigational background and he's a good coxswain."

"I beg to differ, Sir. Sharkey has a wealth of experience, knows every nook and cranny in the gulf and has a good head. If I was out there I would want Sharkey to come and get me," said Tanner.

"Okay! Send Sharkey then!" said the supervisor, shrugging his shoulders.

Tanner picked up the loud hailer.

"Captain Sharkey and crew report to the terminal building immediately."

Sharkey was just about to take a sip from his coffee when the call came through.

"Darn… a man can't even drink his coffee in peace nowadays," he said and began walking towards the terminal with Carlton and Furlonge in tow.

Tanner was waiting outside the door.

"Cap'n Sharkey, I want you and your crew to go to Platform D and pick up three men for me please."

Sharkey recognised the urgency in Tanner's voice and headed towards the Ocean Missile immediately. Carlton scrambled down into the engine room and in a flash had the two GMs barking. The sailor threw off the ropes and Sharkey pointed the Ocean Missile towards the stream. Tanner stood on the pier waving and shouted to Sharkey:

"Have a safe trip now!"

The Ocean Missile left the channel and headed into the open sea which was still eerily calm. Sharkey looked at his watch; it was quarter past the hour of ten. The sky was still an early morning blue, then suddenly, as if someone was using a giant's paint brush, huge portions of the sky began to turn dark grey. Now the painter was mixing some more black into his paint and as if he was really in a hurry, he turned the whole sky grey black. The wind began to blow in little gusts, tracing out little avenues on the water's surface and as the velocity increased the avenues turned into waves.

Back at the base, Tanner was apprehensive. He sat on his chair and nervously drummed his fingers on the desk. A call was coming through on the radio.

"Trident Base, Trident Base, come in to the MET Office. Over."

"Trident Base receiving. Over."

"System has picked up speed and heading westward rapidly. Would make your destination three quarters of an hour earlier. How do you copy me? Over."

"Copy you loud and clear. Over," said Tanner and immediately he radioed Sharkey: "Ocean Missile, Ocean Missile, come in to the Trident Base. Over."

"Ocean Missile receiving. Over."

"Ocean Missile, location please? Over."

"Ten minutes from Platform D. Over."

"The storm would be on you any minute now. Make haste and get out! I repeat. Make haste and get out! Over!"

"Message received and understood. Over," said Sharkey.

White caps were forming on the crest of the waves and the rain began to drizzle. Sharkey could see Platform D off his port bow. The wind began to blow in earnest, the waves getting higher. The sea seemed to be coming up from its depths in great lumps.

As Sharkey approached Platform D, the wind unleashed its naked fury. Objects were flying all over the platform. Sharkey could see the three men leaving the dog house and running towards the boat landing. A sheet of galvanise suddenly lurched from the compressor station, flew across the men's path and the man in front clutched his throat, stumbled, briefly regained his balance but took a heavy fall. The two others shouldered him and dragged him towards the landing.

Sharkey had already spun the Missile and backed in with her stern to the landing. As the Missile came into contact with the structure, Sharkey pushed the throttles to full speed, locking the stern against the landing.

Carlton and Furlonge were already at the aft and as the boat went down into the trough of a wave, they grabbed the injured man and pulled him onto the deck. The vessel went up again on the next wave and as it slammed down again into the trough, the two men dived unto the deck. Immediately, Sharkey pulled back his throttles, engaged forward, pressed down his throttles again and the Missile went flying over the next wave.

Carlton, Furlonge and the two men lifted the injured man into the passenger cabin and laid him on the floor. Carlton got a towel from his bag and placed it around the injured man's neck; blood was everywhere. Sharkey was already on course to Trident Base as the rain came, pouring down. Carlton came into the wheel house.

"How is he?" asked Sharkey.

"Don't look good to me, Skipper. He's losing a lot of blood."

"Darn weather has knocked out the radio." said Sharkey as they ran into a mountainous wave.

The Ocean Missile almost stood on her stern, her bow pointing straight at the sky as if she was going to launch into space, then she came down with a wicked slam-clap that thundered. Sharkey pulled back the throttles. He had to think fast. Under normal circumstances, he was forty-five minutes away from Trident Base but in this type of weather... at least an hour and a bit. There was a hospital one hundred yards from the Cedros beach. If he turned her around and ran with the waves he could be in Cedros in twenty minutes, where he would run the Old Lady aground on the sandy beach. Sharkey's mind was made.

Aggressively, he turned the Ocean Missile around and fixed his course for Cedros. The swells were big, but now the Missile was running with the waves. Up and down she went, squirming as she reached the top of a wave, then she seemed to stand still for just a second, the rudder would give an ominous vibrating rattle, and she would dive, and just when you thought that she was going down, never to return, she would surface slowly, like a creature coming up for air. Then she would plow on again.

They were nearing Cedros in blinding rain. Sharkey's sharp eyes were looking for the point that jutted into the sea, for just beyond it was the sandy beach. He had to be sure. Suddenly, he glimpsed it and he veered to starboard. He travelled about one hundred yards parallel to the coast, and then he faced his bow to the beach, slowed the engines and waited. He saw what he was looking for: a huge wave rushing towards the shore. He pushed his throttle and got onto the crest of the wave. Brace yourselves, he warned, then raced the engines and, with the help of the wave's momentum, got three-quarter of the Missile onto the sandy beach.

Carlton immediately killed the engines while Furlonge and one of the men scrambled over the bow. Debris was flying all around and the fierce winds repressed the shouts of weary men under tremendous pressure. Sharkey and the other man lowered the injured fellow to the pair below, hustled overboard and the four of them, sharing the weight of the wounded man, ran without stopping to the hospital, Carlton sprinting behind. The men almost broke down the door before the nurses and the doctor opened it.

The doctor snapped into action, stabilising the patient and stemming the flow of blood. When the patient was resting comfortably, the doctor went into the waiting room.

"How is he doing, Doc?" asked Sharkey.

"He is resting comfortably. You got here just in time; another ten minutes and he might have been a goner."

"Thank goodness," sighed Sharkey.

"You boys look soaked to the bone!" the doctor shouted, trying to get above the noise of the wind. "Appears you can all use a cup of coffee!"

Sharkey smiled and shouted back:

"I was wondering if you would never ask!"

The next day the Trident Base Port Engineer inspected her on the beach. Eventually a tug boat came and towed her out to sea, heading to the docks in Port of Spain. There was some superficial damage to the hull, two bent propeller shafts and two damaged propellers. The Trident Base Port Engineer cursed Sharkey bitterly for his heroics:

"Look what you gone and do we best f-ing boat!"

Sharkey looked him from head to toe and calmly concluded:

"Mr. Weeks, when I work on a vessel my priorities will always be in this order: one: life; two: limb, and then property. There is nothing that you can ever do or say to change that."

Then he walked away.

Mr. Weeks continued to rant and rave, kicking away an empty bucket that was standing at the side of the Missile, but deep down inside he knew that Sharkey had made the right decision.

Quick Silva

Tears trickled down Pedro's cheeks as his father walked him to his new school.

"Why you crying for?" asked Randy Persad.

"Ah stone gone in me eye," he lied.

"Stone gone in you eye? I don't know why the hell your mother send you quite San Fernando to school for! She think up here is Icacos? Well let me tell you, up here is dog eat dog, so done with yuh cry-cry stupidness."

"Okay, Pa."

"And don't call me Pa! You stepmother ain't want nobody to know I is you father. She tell the neighbours you is my nephew so from now on, I is Uncle Randy to you."

Pedro started to cry again.

"Look boy, hush you tail, you hear me. I up to my neck ketching my arse all the time and as thing start to look a little bright, yuh mother pull this on me."

"She only want good for me, and besides, when she put Sando school on the paper she never thought I'd ah pass for it," Pedro stated.

"But it have good schools in Point Fortin and that plenty closer to Icacos, is only revenge she looking for you know."

"Mammy not like that. She only looking for betterment for me."

"Oh hush you mouth, you don't know woman yet, they like revenge too bad. She hear me and the wife going good, so she send she little envoy to mash up we living."

"What is an envoy, Sir?" Pedro asked.

"Oh go to hell. You pass Common Entrance and you don't know what is a envoy. Anyway, look the gate for Sando Sec. right there. I turning back from here... you could find you way back home?"

"Yes, Sir."

"I late for work. Look a fifty-cents piece. See what you could do with that."

Randy turned and hurried off in the opposite direction.

Pedro dried his tears and walked through the gate, utterly lost and looking quite the same. All the boys he saw were decked off in bellbottom pants, flaring out at the ankles. Pedro had on a pants with pleats that clung to his ankles, a style of a long-gone era that they referred to as gun mouths, and as he passed by a group of boys, one shouted:

"Aye! Look a skeleton in a gun mouth pants!"

The other boys in the group laughed heartily.

The tears welled up in Pedro's eyes once more and when he passed another group of boys, they started mocking him, shouting:

"Pow! Potow! Pow!"

The rivers burst their banks and the tears streamed down his face. An announcement came over the P.A. System, asking all form one students to assemble in the auditorium in ten minutes. Pedro dried his eyes and followed other students to the large hall where boys and girls were forming into little groups and chatting. Pedro stood by himself, because he didn't know anyone, but suddenly a strange, little fellow, with hair that stuck up straight like wire pickers, approached him.

"What you name?" he asked.

"I name Pedro Silva."

"Me's Satesh. Whey you from?"

"Icacos."

"That sound like real country side place, boy."

"How you know that?"

"Because you look like country-bookie to me."

"And you?" asked Pedro.

"Me's country-bookie too, from Barrackpore. You have *gyul?*"

"I too young for gyul, I only have twelve years," said Pedro.

"I twelve too, but I have gyul since I nine, she name was Shanmatie but we break up last year."

"So you don't have any now?" asked Pedro.

"Boy, how you so chupid? You expect man like me not to have gyul. I have a next one now, she name Basanti. She live right next door to me. Talk 'bout gyul could sing Indian song and she could make roti too. Soon as I finish school we going to marry."

Pedro looked at Satesh to see if he was joking, but he was dead serious. A bell sounded and a teacher came into the auditorium and made the form one students line up before the head table. The principal, a stern, square-jawed, heavyset man came and stood at the table. He looked like a bulldog standing on its hind legs.

"Good morning, my little ones," he said. Then he rattled off a list of do's and don'ts, followed by a string of threats from beatings, to suspensions, to expulsions, to any new students who might be inclined towards the don'ts. Then he called to a teacher who was standing at the door of the auditorium: "Bring in the culprit," and the teacher brought in a boy, who might have been a form three student, and took him before the headmaster. "This young fellow cursed a teacher on the last day of school. Maybe he thought that the long summer holidays would have buried the matter." And with that, he took a guava whip from the table and planted three solid ones on the young fellow's back, whose upper body writhed like a snake under the impact. "This is just to let you newcomers know that no wrongdoing escapes Clyde Watson."

By now, every student in the room knew that their parents had made a mistake in choosing schools for them. The next speaker was the dean. He came up to the table with a whip in his hand. He was a tall, skinny man whose pant's waist was buckled up almost to his chest. When he smiled, his teeth looked like fangs and somehow, he quite resembled a Doberman.

"I am Dave Ramsook, your Dean of Discipline. I have been entrusted with the portfolio of enforcing discipline. I and my good partner here, *Mr. Screeler*–" and he raised the whip he held and shook it menacingly – "aim to make sure, that you all understand the true meaning of the word discipline."

Satesh touched Pedro's arm and whispered:

"Like is only haters running this school, boy!"

"You there!" Ramsook barked, pointing, with *Mr. Screeler*, in the direction of Satesh and Pedro.

A fellow standing in front of Pedro, pointed to himself and asked:

"Me, Sir?"

"No! Not you! The skinny fellow behind you!"

"Me?" asked Pedro.

"Yes you! Come up here."

Pedro went up to the table.

"Why were you speaking back there?" barked Ramsook.

"I didn't speaking, Sir."

"You are lying!"

"I not lying, Sir."

"Then you are saying that I am lying?"

"You not lying either, Sir."

"Then you admit! Turn around!"

Whatap! Whap!

Mr. Screeler collided with Pedro's skinny back and he began to cry again.

"Now get back to your position! And you my little friends, get this through your thick skulls: you do the crime, you make the time. *Mr. Screeler* and I, we will be watching you."

Mr. Ramsook did a sort of dance and he sauntered off.

After the assembly, they were shown to their classes and although Satesh had landed Pedro his first licking, he was hoping that they would be placed in the same class. It wasn't to be; Satesh was placed in Form 1:2 and Pedro went further down the corridor to 1:4. They entered their classes and Pedro rested his head on the desk and shut out his surroundings. It was half an hour later when their form teacher, Mrs. Davies, came into 1:4 to address her class.

"Good morning, students," she said.

"Good morning, Miss," the class chorused.

"I am sorry to be late, but we just had a meeting in the staff room with the principal. Please stand and step into the columns between your desks."

The class complied and Mrs. Davies walked between the students, went back to the front of the class and sat on her chair.

"You may all sit now," she said and pointed towards Pedro. "Young man, could you step forward please?"

Pedro got up, his knees buckling as he walked to the front, wondering what he had done this time.

"This!" Mrs. Davies exclaimed, "is how all the boys in the class should be dressed. When your parents came to the orientation, they were specifically given slips of paper with the school's dress code. On that paper it was clearly written that the boys' trousers were to be pleated at the top and narrow at the ankles."

A loud murmur went up in the classroom. A little fellow stood and said:

"But Miss, that not in-style!"

"Sit down! and be quiet! School is not about style. You came here to get an education. Is that understood?"

"Yes, Miss," they answered.

"Now you all have one week to alter those pants at the ankles, and you girls, it was clearly stated that your skirts should drop lower than your knees. You also have one week to make these adjustments and come Monday morning, anyone who is dressed contrary to the code will be sent home. Is that understood?"

"Yes, Miss!"

"Young man, why are you crying?"

"Ah not crying, Miss," said Pedro wiping his eyes.

"Okay, son, you can go back to your seat now."

Mrs. Davies went on speaking for a while, then she started taking questions from the children and when she was finished, the recess bell rang. The children rushed out of the classroom; some headed to the canteen, others to the playing field and some to look for their friends in other classrooms. Pedro, however, remained alone with his head on his desk. When he heard footsteps, he looked up; it was Satesh.

"I real sorry 'bout this morning," he said.

"Is okay," said Pedro.

"Nah, I should ah be big man and say was me who was talking, but the truth is I didn't want no part of *Mr. Screeler*, boy."

Pedro managed a smile.

Satesh pushed his hand into his pants pocket and came out with a sugar cake wrapped in brown paper. "Take piece," Satesh said and Pedro broke off a piece and placed it in his mouth.

"Mmm… taste good."

"Must taste good, boy, my Ma make the best sugar cake in all Barrackpore."

They spoke for a while and then the bell rang. Before Satesh left he asked:

"You not vex with me then?"

"No I not vex."

"Ah did done know that a'ready," said Satesh.

"And how that so?" asked Pedro.

"Cause big man doh vex with one another," Satesh explained and rushed off to class.

During the lunch break, Pedro went to the canteen, bought a *rockcake* and a bottled soft drink for his lunch and went back to his class and ate. Shortly after, he was joined by Satesh who informed him that two newcomers had made their acquaintance with *Mr. Screeler*. Apparently, they were caught fighting during recess and were sent to the dean's office. The remainder of the day passed quietly and after school, Pedro made his way back to where his father and stepmother lived. When he reached the house, his stepmother was speaking to the next-door neighbour through the wire-mesh fence. She said:

"I have to go now, Neighbour Rosy, Randy nephew come. He from Icacos but he pass Common Entrance for San Fernando school, so he staying by we."

The neighbour looked at Pedro and said:

"But look how he resemble Randy in truth… family can't hide nah. He just fairer but he is the image of Randy."

Vijanti face got long and her lips pursed, then she relaxed and said:

"See you later, neighbour." As soon as they were inside the house she barked: "You see this shit! I don't know why your mother couldn't keep she little bastard for sheself. She only send you here to mash up me and Randy living."

Then she held on to her belly. Her loose dress clung to her and Pedro realised that his stepmother was very pregnant. She began to cry softly and said:

"Look at me! Belly big with he chile, and now he bring he bastard to done kill me. Look you food on the table *eh*. Eat when you ready!"

Pedro looked at the food but hunger had deserted him. He went into the little room, placed his books on the table, took off his shoes and lay on the bed. He felt sorry for himself. The events of the last couple of days kept running through his mind. It was clear to him now, that his mother had chosen a San Fernando school for two reasons. She wanted the best for him but she also had another reason up her sleeve. Mootilal was his mother's boy friend of the last two years; he and Pedro never got along.

"Send the boy by his father, Louisa," he would say, "and you would see how nice me and you would live."

It was clear that she had chosen this opportunity to get rid of him and please Mootilal. Pedro, in his little mind, felt cornered. Clearly he was not wanted in San Fernando either. He did not want to cause any friction between his father and stepmother, he was afraid of the atmosphere at Sando Sec. and he wanted no further part of *Mr. Screeler*. He made up his mind: he would quit school when he got back home. His mother had made arrangements for her brother Felix to pick him up at the end of the coming week to spend the weekend in Icacos. When he got home, he would tell her he was not going back to school. As to his future, he was not worried. He would be a fisherman; there were already a lot of twelve-year-old fishermen in Icacos.

When Randy came home from work, it was almost dark. He hung his cap on a nail in the kitchen.

"The boy reach home?" he asked.

"Yes, he in he room," said Vijanti.

"I hungry, gyul. Whey my food?"

"It on the table," said Vijanti.

"Buh wait, who this other plate a food belong to?" asked Randy.

"The boy," said Vijanti.

"He ain't eat yet?" asked Randy.

"No, I begging he all the time to eat, buh like he not hungry," said Vijanti.

"Pedro!" called Randy.

"I coming, Sir," answered Pedro and as he came into the kitchen, Vijanti started to fuss over him:

"Sit down and eat with you father nah, son," she pleaded.

"I not feeling hungry," said Pedro.

"Look boy, not so to answer you aunty! You suppose to say: I not feeling hungry, Aunty."

"Oh leave the boy, Randy, he only ah chile you know," said Vijanti.

"Well suit you-self boy, but remember, man mus never make style on food, especially when they hungry."

Pedro went back to his room.

As soon as Randy had finished eating and had gone to take a bath, Vijanti went into Pedro's room:

"You nasty little bitch! You better go and eat you blasted food. You trying to make you father feel I starving you?"

Pedro said nothing.

The next day, Pedro went to school and kept to himself. He hardly walked about because there was always someone waiting to tease him about his pants. Satesh came to visit him at lunch time and he asked:

"You see the French teacher, Miss Leiba?"

"Yes," replied Pedro.

"Boy, that is a nice gyul eh?"

"You mad! That a big lady to you!" exclaimed Pedro.

"Big lady? Boy, if wasn't for my Basanti, I make Miss Leiba my wife in two-twos."

That evening when Pedro got home, his stepmother went immediately and took out his lunch.

"Look you food eh, boy."

Pedro was hungry so he ate.

After, his stepmother sat there speaking to herself:

"I waiting for Randy to come to pick a coconut for me. I feeling to drink coconut water."

Then she began to wash the dishes. Pedro went quietly into the backyard, climbed the tallest tree, like a squirrel, and shook down a bunch of coconuts. He came down, went into the kitchen, took a cutlass, peeled one of the coconuts and gave it to his stepmother.

"This for me?" she asked.

"Yes, Aunty," said Pedro and she drank it.

"You didn't fraid you fall?" she asked.

"No, Aunty. Is all we Icacos boys does do. Climb coconut tree whole day."

Monday morning there was a call to general assembly and all the students huddled in the auditorium. Mr. Watson and Mr. Ramsook were presiding at the table, while the rest of the staff formed a semicircle behind them. Mrs. Davies was called upon to offer a word of prayer and then Mr. Watson got down to business. He turned to his staff:

"Mr. Reginald and Mr. Seerattan, I want you both to stand by the exits of the auditorium and make sure that no student leaves." Then he turned to the students: "Last week Monday, masters and mistresses of all forms passed information to the students concerning the school's dress code. They would have also told you about certain alterations to be made. Would you all oblige and form yourselves into lines so Mr. Ramsook and I can carry out an inspection."

Twenty-one fishes were snared in Operation Dress Code and Mr. Watson lined them up in front of the assembly.

"Is there anyone of you, for some reason or the other, who did not know of these instructions?" Mr. Watson asked.

A fellow in the line stepped forward and raised his hand.

"Yes!" Mr. Watson snapped, pointing his whip at the fellow.

"Sir, I was not in school for the whole of last week," the student said.

"And why is that so?" asked Mr. Watson.

"I went New York on a holiday and I miss my flight, Sir."

Mr. Reginald, who was manning one of the exits, raised his hand.

"What is it, Mr. Reginald?" Mr. Watson enquired.

"Student is lying, Sir, I saw him selling nuts on High Street last Monday... I myself bought a pack off him."

The assembly erupted in laughter.

"What is your name, student?" Mr. Watson bellowed.

"David Augustine, Sir."

"Well Mr. Augustine, you will bring in your parents tomorrow morning for us to discuss your flight arrangements. The rest of you are suspended for three days, beginning today. You would report back on Thursday morning accompanied by your parents. Assembly dismissed!"

Mr. Ramsook walked away with his fangs bared, *Mr. Screeler* tucked under his arm, disappointed that he and his partner hadn't been summoned to action.

Thursday, during the lunch break, Satesh and Pedro were chatting when two form five students peeped into the classroom and entered.

"That's him!" said one of the boys.

"Which one? The picker-hair one?" asked the other.

"Nah, the tall, *magaar* one. He is the stupid, country-bookie bitch who waltz in here last Monday morning with he gun-mouth pants like if he just come out the eighteen century. Is he that have all ah we wearing gun-mouths now."

"You know what you cause, young boy?" asked the other.

"No," replied Pedro.

"Well I will tell you. I had a nice *reds* going Convent, over a year now we going good and bam! Just so this week I lost she. You know why I lost she?"

"No."

"Well I will tell you. Because of you, they pass a order for everyone to turn they pants gun-mouth and I comply. Then I went up by my gyul school Tuesday to look for she. She friends see me coming and they say, 'Colleen, look ah old man in a gun mouth pants come to look for you.' Right there

Colleen dump me like a hot potato. And you know what I see yesterday?"

"No," said Pedro.

"I see Colleen, waltzing down High Street after school with a Naps man. If you see the fellar, sharp like a razor, decked out in his nice, bellbottomed pants, holding hands with my gyul and I stand up there like Sad Sack in my gun-mouth pants. Thanks to you, all I have now is Miss Palmer. You know who is Miss Palmer?" he asked.

"No," said Pedro.

Whatap!

The slap collided perfectly with Pedro's profile and immediately he began to cry.

"You have just been struck by Miss Palmer," he said, holding up his right palm, "and if you utter a word about this episode to anyone I will reintroduce you to Miss Palmer."

"And that goes for you too, you little, picker-hair bitch," said the first to Satesh and he and his partner walked out of the classroom.

Pedro was now sobbing uncontrollably and Satesh tried to console him.

"Take ease padner, it could ah be worse."

"You don't know Satesh, my mother don't want me, my father don't like me and nobody in this school don't like me either," Pedro sobbed.

"Doh say that, Pedro. Remember I, Satesh from Barrackpore, is yuh padner."

"When I go home this weekend, I not coming back to school again," Pedro admitted.

"Doh give up so easy, padner. You know Carol Nurse from my class? She mother and father dead in accident same day she sit Common Entrance and she ain't give up. She coming to school as normal."

Pedro dried his eyes as Satesh left and children filtered into the classroom for the afternoon period.

Friday afternoon, as planned, Pedro's Uncle Felix picked him up and took him to Icacos. Louisa had prepared her son's favorite: curried crabs and cassava dumplings and he and Uncle Felix did justice to his mother's tasty cooking. When Uncle Felix left for his home, Pedro said to Louisa:

"Ma, I not going back to school."

"Boy! You crazy?" asked Louisa.

"Nah Ma, I done make up my mind. I not going back!"

"So what you going to do for ah living?" asked Louisa.

"I going to be a fisherman."

"Fisherman? You must be mad! Is whole month Mootilal working in the sea and all he make is six dollars. You think when you get big you could mind wife and children on that?"

"But Ma, you don't understand, I go dead if I go back... is only licks I getting up there."

"Don't tell me that son-of-a-bitch Randy hitting you!"

"Nah!"

"Who? You stepmother?"

"No, not she."

"Then who hitting you, boy?" asked Louisa.

"The people in the school, Ma."

"What people in the school?"

Pedro started to cry.

"Okay son, okay, tell mammy all about it," she said, embracing him.

Pedro dried his eyes.

"Is the teachers and the students, Ma. They take *unvantage* on me."

"Go ahead, son, tell me what they do."

"You know how people does give cat and dog name, Ma? Imagine a big man give ah whip ah name. He call it *Mr. Screeler* and he beat me for nothing first day a school."

"Who is this big man with *Mr. Screeler*, son?"

"Mr. Ramsook, Ma. He is the dean... the man does beat children not because he want to correct them, but because he love to beat."

"Son... that is a big school you know and in order to maintain discipline the teachers have to be strict."

"But I was innocent, Ma."

"It does happen sometimes, son."

"And one day I and my padner liming in my class and two, big fellars come in and one slap me in my face."

"For what?"

"Because he gyul leave he."

"You come like you father now... you taking away people gyul?"

"No Ma, he say he gyul leave he because I cause him to have to wear gun-mouth pants to school and a fellar with a bellbottom pants take way he gyul."

"Buh wat jail is this ah hearing! He gyul must be leave he because he damn thing dead!"

"Ah doh want to go back, Ma. Please?"

"Pedro, I want you to listen to me carefully. You know how much children in this village wish they did pass Common Entrance? You know what I do when I hear you pass? I say thank you God for giving my son a chance to educate he-self so he could get away from the sea and won't have to slave in the coconut estates when he get big. Doh give up now son, have courage."

When his mother was finished, Pedro knew that he would have to go back.

Monday morning, during the recess break, while Pedro was sitting all by himself, Satesh came and peeped into the classroom. When he saw Pedro, a big smile broke out on his face. He rushed up to Pedro and placed his arms around him.

"Boy, you had me worried. I thought I would *ah* never see you again. I tell my Basanti and she tell me 'doh worry ah sure he mother go talk sense in he head.' But boy, I did still worried."

"Is true boy, ah come back for my mother sake."

"Remember the fellar who slap you?"

Pedro nodded.

"I find out he name. He name Dale Thomas, an he in 5:1. I tell my father and he say if he trouble we again to just tell him and he will send one of his cane cutters to *planass* his *arse* after school."

In the second month, Randy showed Pedro a shortcut that he could take on his way to and from school, a big concrete canal that passed just behind San Fernando Sec. The canal continued and passed just about fifty yards from their home. By taking this route, Pedro would be able to reduce the three-quarters-of-a-mile walk, to half-a-mile. A few days later, Pedro was coming home, after school, along the canal and as he rounded a bend, he saw a Rastafarian man smoking a long, funny-looking cigarette. The man did not see him until he was very close and he became quite startled and hurriedly swallowed the cigarette.

"*Jeezus*! Boy, you almost make me jump out of my skin," said the Rastafarian.

"I sorry."

"Oh is alright. I thought was Babylon. Whey you from?"

"Icacos."

"What! You a long ways from home, boy."

"Yes, but I staying in San Fernando."

"Okay… you know ah man down Icacos name George Slinger?"

"You mean the fellow that does sell birds?" asked Pedro.

"Yes, the Bird Man."

"Yes! I know him. He live 'bout half mile from me."

The Rastafarian shaded his eyes with the palm of his right hand.

"Look up on that hill there," he said.

Pedro turned and saw a little house standing on the hill. Vegetables grew all around it, in neat rows. A woman was standing in front of the house.

"You see my Empress up there? Give she a lil wave," the Rastafarian said.

Pedro raised his hand and waved, and the woman, dressed in an iridescent dress and green head tie, waved back.

"That's my wife, Empress Naomi. They call me Ras Lessy," he beamed and pushed out a big, strong hand to Pedro.

They shook hands and Pedro said:

"I name Pedro."

"What! A nice, Spanish name, boy! But you look more like *ah* Indian to me!"

"My mother mix with Spanish and negro, an' my father is ah Indian," said Pedro.

"What! You is a real callaloo. I myself have a drop of Spanish blood but I's ninety-five percent African. Anyway, whenever you pass by, you must come up the hill and check us out, man. Now run along before your folks get worried."

The next afternoon, when Pedro was coming from school, Ras Lessy was waiting for him.

"Aye, is you! What happening, man?" he asked.

"I okay," said Pedro.

"I want you to come up and meet my Empress."

"Well… okay… but I can't stay long," said Pedro.

They went up the hill and Lessy introduced him to his wife, Empress Naomi. She was beautiful. They sat in a little shed at the side of the house, the cleanest surroundings Pedro had ever seen. Empress Naomi went inside, came back with three glasses of orange juice and a sweetbread, cut up into pieces, on a waiter, and passed it to Pedro and her husband. They enquired of Icacos, his family and how he happened to be coming to a school that was so far from his home. Then the Empress said:

"Lessy and I have been married for fifteen years."

"You have any children?" Pedro asked.

"Nah, we still practising," Lessy joked.

"Oh Lessy, you must not talk such foolishness in front of the child," the Empress censured.

Lessy laughed again but there was a touch of sadness in their eyes.

"Come let me show you my garden, man," Lessy said, and he began to walk Pedro through the neat rows of vegetables.

"This is what I do for a living. I plant the land and sell my crops in the market."

"Is hard work?" asked Pedro.

"Yes, but I enjoy it. I work hard all day and in the evening I bathe an go down by the canal to relax and have ah lil smoke."

"I have to go now," said Pedro.

"Okay… but don't forget to look we up," Lessy said, as they walked back to the shed.

Pedro thanked the Empress for her kindness.

"Okay son, but remember you welcome anytime," she said.

Lessy walked him down to the canal and waved to him as he went his way. When Pedro got home, only his father was there.

"Well boy, looks like you going to get a brother or sister anytime now," Randy said.

"Where Aunty?"

"She take in with pain 'bout twelve o'clock. Good thing I was off today. I take she to the hospital. Look I put a sandwich on the table for you."

"Thanks," said Pedro and he began eating the sandwich.

"I going back to the hospital now. You could make out by yourself?"

"Yes, Sir," replied Pedro.

"I don't know what time I coming back, but make sure to bathe and lock up good when you going to sleep."

"Okay, you go tell Aunty hello for me."

Randy came back about eleven that night with the news that Pedro had a little brother. Pedro smiled sleepily and went back to bed.

The next day, he gave Satesh the good news and in the afternoon when he reached home and heard the cries of his little brother, he ran into the house excitedly. Vijanti allowed him to pet the baby. He was tiny and kind of red all over. They named him Ringo.

"But how he so small?" asked Pedro.

"You was small just like that when you born too," said Randy.

The next day Vijanti wrapped baby Ringo in a blanket and went to the fence to introduce him to Neighbour Rosy.

"Eh, Eh, another young Randy," said Neighbour Rosy.

"Another young Randy?"

"Yes neighbour… another young Randy. You thought I would not find out? I know Pedro is Randy son. I have friends everywhere you know. I don't know how allyuh young people so deceitful."

"I sorry, neighbour, but I was too embarrass to tell you," Vijanti confessed.

"I want to tell you something though. Be careful of the boy mother, eh. Them countryside people know a lot a obeah."

Christmas holidays came and Pedro returned to Icacos. It was a wonderful time. Reunited with his old primary school friends, he went roaming the village, bathing in the sea and playing games with them. His mother prepared all sorts of tasty dishes and it was a reluctant Pedro that returned to San Fernando Secondary in January. Gradually, he started to fit into the Sando life. He still kept to himself at school. Satesh was his only true friend. The other children still laughed at him and teased him, but the afternoons offered a lot more now. He looked forward to his meetings with Ras Lessy and his Empress, and he hurried home after to play with his little brother, who had discovered the art of smiling.

Events in the month of February brought about a change in Pedro's status at San Fernando Sec.; the cricket season had started. 1:3 and 1:4 had their Physical Education periods together and that lasted the entire Friday mornings. The form master of 1:3, Mr. Reginald, who was also the school's sport master, was a cricket fanatic and he asked Mrs. Davies to allow the boys of 1:4 to play a cricket match against his boys. During the game Pedro was given a chance to bowl and there was not a batsman from 1:3 who could stand up to the pace of the tall, skinny country-bookie. 1:4 won the match and Pedro was the toast of his class.

He was given the nickname *Quick Silva*.

Whenever he passed around the other form one boys, they would point to him, saying:

"That is the fast bowler who mash up 1:3."

Ras Lessy and the Empress quizzed Pedro and found out that his birthday was on the 12th of March, and on that day, when Pedro was walking home, they called out to him. When he went up to the shed, Empress Naomi came outside with a birthday cake and thirteen lighting candles which she made Pedro blow out. Then Ras Lessy gave him a present wrapped in gift paper. Pedro was elated. After they cut the cake and had a few pieces, the Empress put the rest in a box and gave it to him to carry home. When Pedro got home, Vijanti wanted to know where he had gotten the cake from. Pedro told her that the Rastafarian and his wife, who lived on the hill over the canal, had made it for his birthday. Vijanti flew into a rage and said:

"So you begging people to make cake for your birthday now? You couldn't tell me and you father it was your birthday? And I coulda make a cake for you!"

She flung the cake into the dustbin. When Randy came home, Vijanti told him about the cake.

"You shouldn't do that," Randy said, "everybody around here know that the Rastafarian and his wife is nice people."

The following Friday, Mr. Reginald challenged Mrs. Davies class to another cricket game. This time, Pedro was given a new ball to open the bowling. Lessy, who was on his way home from the market, was passing right above the San Fernando Sec. cricket ground and when he saw it was Pedro who was bowling, he put down his basket and sat down on a stump. He was amazed at the speed of his little friend's deliveries. He called out and Pedro waved back. That afternoon, after school, an excited Ras Lessy was waiting for him in the canal.

"You never told me you was a fast bowler."

"I use to play a little bit for my school in Icacos," Pedro grinned back.

"You have some potential there, boy. I use to be a fast bowler myself you know. I does do a little coaching with the Oxford Youths on a Saturday. If you come to Skinner Park I could enroll you in the club sessions."

Pedro spoke to Randy and obtained permission, and Saturday morning, he went to Skinner Park where Lessy enrolled him. Saturday after Saturday, Lessy worked on his young charges, paying special attention to his little friend Pedro.

Easter holidays came and Pedro returned to Icacos. He told his mother about Ras Lessy and the Empress and how good they were to him. His mother gave him some money to buy presents for them. He bought a lovely, red head tie for the Empress but had no idea what to buy for Lessy so he sought the advice of his friend Tabby who asked him:

"What the Rasta-man like?"

"Is two things I know he likes," Pedro stated flatly, "He like to plant and he like to smoke weed."

"Well, why you don't buy some good weed for the man?" asked Tabby.

"I don't know whey they does sell that!"

"Give me the money and I would get some for you," Tabby offered.

The next day Tabby brought some weed, wrapped up in a brown paper, and gave it to Pedro.

"Hide it good and don't let nobody see it."

On the first day of the new term, when Pedro was coming home from school, he went up the hill to visit Ras Lessy and the Empress. He gave her the red head tie and she gave him a big hug, then he took the little, brown package out of his pocket and gave it to Ras Lessy. When he opened the package, he almost collapsed.

"Whey you get this thing from, boy?" he asked.

"I buy it in Icacos," Pedro admitted.

"Boy, you don't know this illegal? You could ah get lock up for carrying this around."

"I wanted to buy something for you and I always seeing you smoking this, so I buy it," said Pedro.

"Jesus… son, look at the kind of trouble I could ah put you in. Naomi, you hear what going on here?" Lessy said.

"I always tell you to stop smoking that craziness. Look at the kind ah trouble you could of get the child in," Naomi scolded.

Lessy took the weed, threw it away and he never smoked *herbs* in his life again.

When Pedro got home that evening, he rushed into the room to play with his little brother and as he touched his face, the child began to wail.

"What you do him?" asked Vijanti.

"I just touch his face, Aunty," Pedro replied innocently.

A little while after, the baby started to vomit. Vijanti went to the fence and called out to her neighbour who came running: Rosy asked:

"What is it, Vijanti?"

"Pedro just come from school and touch the chile and the chile start to cry and vomit just so."

"You sure the boy mother ain't give he some kind of nastiness to touch the child with? I done tell you about these country people and they obeah."

"Oh God! Oh God! My child will dead," said Vijanti and she ran into the house and started to beat Pedro with a broom stick, saying: "You come here with your blasted obeah from you mother and want to kill my child."

Neighbour Rosy came over and said:

"Vijanti, you best carry the child to *jaray* by the priest up de road and see if he could ward off the evil spirits."

Randy arrived from work around the same time and Vijanti gave him the story. Randy said:

"You must not believe in this kinda foolishness."

Neighbour Rosy cut in:

"Randy, I older than you, boy. Take the child by the priest to *jaray*."

Randy turned to Pedro.

"And why the ass you touch the child for?"

"I was only playing with him, Sir," Pedro sobbed.

Randy and Vijanti took the child to the priest who *jarayed* him. When they came back, the child continued vomiting during the night and showed signs of diarrhea. The next morning Vijanti said:

"Is yuh ex-gyul, Randy, she send something with the boy to harm the chile."

Randy, in his frustrations, bought into Vijanti's insinuations, awoke Pedro and started to beat him. Pedro escaped from him, ran out of the house, all the way to Ras Lessy and gave him the story.

"But what kind of stupid man is this to believe in this kind of foolishness?" He accompanied Pedro back home and called out to Randy who came outside. "Why you ill-treating the little boy for?"

"If you know what he do, you wouldn't ask me that," Randy retorted.

"But this is a modern world, how a big man like you could believe in this sort of superstition? Take my advice: take the child to a doctor immediately. Stop making yourself a fool and let the boy get ready and go to school."

Randy and Vijanti took the child to Dr. Singh who enquired:

"What is wrong with the baby?"

Vijanti started to relate to the doctor how her stepson had brought some kind of obeah from his mother in Icacos, touched the child with it and immediately after, the child started vomiting and showed signs of diarrhea. Dr. Singh held up his hands and said:

"Wait. I refuse to think that there are still people as ignorant as you in this world. Let me see the child."

Vijanti passed the child to the doctor and after a thorough examination, he said to them:

"This child is suffering from gastroenteritis. It is a disease that is caused by flies. We would have to ward him in the hospital for a couple of days."

"He not in any great danger then?" Randy asked.

"Well I'll leave out the great," the doctor advised. Then he turned to Vijanti. "Did you ill-treat your stepson because of your superstitious beliefs?"

Vijanti nodded.

"Then I suggest that you apologise to him when you get home," he said and gave them the letter of admittance to the hospital.

During the day, Ras Lessy and the Empress were uneasy.

"Imagine how this man ill-treating the boy and is fifteen years now we praying to have one," Lessy inveighed.

"Instead of the child seeing trouble like that, why we don't ask them for him to stay with us?" Naomi wondered aloud.

"Girl, I would love that, but Indian is funny people. They don't like niggers like we interfering in their business. The next thing we ask them and they stop the boy from coming by us altogether."

"Is true," the wife concurred.

When Pedro was coming from school that afternoon, they were waiting for him.

"You want us to walk you home?" Lessy extended.

"I don't know," Pedro said dolefully.

"I think is a good idea for us to walk you home today, Pedro, but first, let's go up the hill and have something to eat," Naomi said.

After, they walked him home but when they got there, no one was around. The three of them sat on the pavement talking and a little while after, Randy and Vijanti came from the hospital.

"How the baby?" Lessy asked, standing to greet them.

"They keep him in the hospital," Randy and Vijanti said simultaneously.

"But he okay?"

"Yes, he doing a lot better. Allyuh come inside and sit awhile," Randy invited.

"Okay," Lessy and Naomi said hurriedly.

"Listen, I know that you all have been looking out for Pedro a while now and I want to thank you for that. I guess me and the wife been messing up the fellar life of late."

"He's a nice child," Lessy smiled.

"Vijanti, go and get something for the people to drink," Randy said.

"Is okay. You don't have to trouble yourselves," Naomi declined.

"Is no trouble," said Vijanti and she went off to the kitchen.

"We only come to find out 'bout the baby and make sure that everything would be alright with Pedro," Lessy said, still looking for an opening.

"We get kind of confuse and Vijanti was listening to some kind of stupid talk from the neighbour, but the doctor put all that to rest now," Randy added.

"You must have faith in god. Everything will be alright with the baby," Naomi said, nodding at her husband.

Vijanti returned with five glasses of soft drinks on a waiter and passed them around.

"I glad you send him to the cricket sessions on a Saturday," Lessy contributed, looking for another avenue.

"So how he progressing?" asked Randy.

"What I can tell you, is that he is the fastest bowler we have in his age group."

Pedro smiled.

"We have to be going now before it get dark. I hope the baby feel better," Naomi said.

"Thanks. I myself have to go back to the hospital to spend the night with the chile," said Vijanti.

When the Lessy's departed, Randy said to Vijanti:

"Remember the doctor told you something to say to Pedro."

Vijanti started to cry and said through her deep sobs:

"I sorry for ill-treating you, Pedro... I really sorry."

Baby Ringo spent three days in the hospital and came home weak, but smiling, however Pedro was afraid to go near him. After two days, Vijanti said:

"Is all right for you to play with him, you know, Pedro."

Pedro was still apprehensive, but after a while, the smile of little Ringo drew him.

The summer holidays were now upon Pedro and before he left for Icacos, Ras Lessy said to him:

"Remember son, every chance you get, you swim in the sea because it will build your muscles and make you bowl faster."

When Pedro returned to school in September, he was promoted to form 2:4. When Lessy saw him the first evening after school, he could not believe his eyes. He had grown a couple inches taller and his skinny body was now covered by a few pounds of muscles.

"Like all you did during the holidays was swim and eat," Lessy joked.

"Well you told me to swim and mammy made me eat," said Pedro.

"Nice, nice, now we going to get down to some serious cricket, but you must not forget you school work also," Lessy warned.

When they went up the hill, Naomi was twice as surprised.

"But look at how big my son get!" she exclaimed.

One day in December, Randy came home smiling. Pedro was playing with baby Ringo on the bed and Vijanti was folding baby clothes and putting them into the wardrobe draw.

"Girl, I get the breakthrough I always hoping for," he said to Vijanti.

"Let me guess, you getting promotion," she said.

"How you know that?" he asked.

"Because you does be always talking 'bout that."

"Yes gyul, they want a operator in Curepe from January and they offer me the post."

"But that is a long way from Sando," she said.

"Well, I will start to travel in the beginning and then we will look for a place up there to rent," he said.

"But what about, Pedro?" she asked.

"I will have to discuss it with his mother," said Randy.

The next day, Pedro gave Lessy and the Empress the news. Lessy looked at Naomi and their eyes brightened.

"Pedro, you think your mother will allow you to stay with us?" asked Naomi.

"You will have to ask her, Aunty," replied Pedro.

"I think we will have to pay a visit to Icacos," said Lessy.

"Might not be a bad idea to have a talk with Randy first," said Naomi.

The next day Naomi went to High Street and purchased a suit for baby Ringo and in the afternoon she and Lessy accompanied Pedro home. Randy was sitting under the coconut tree with a bottle of rum, having a few celebratory drinks by himself when Lessy and Naomi arrived with Pedro. Vijanti greeted them at the gate and Naomi gave her the present for baby Ringo. She took Naomi into the house and Pedro followed them. Randy called out to Lessy:

"Come and take one with me, Ras, I celebrating."

"Congratulations, I hear 'bout the promotion from Pedro," said Lessy.

"What! News travelling fast, boy!" said Randy.

"Yes, you know the boy proud of you and I glad for you too, man," said Lessy.

"Vijanti, bring a glass for the gentleman please!" shouted Randy.

Lessy accepted the glass and poured a drink into it. Randy replenished his and Lessy made a toast:

"To the promotion, man," and they knocked glasses and downed the contents.

"I really appreciate how you and the Madame does keep an eye on the boy for me," said Randy.

"Is a real pleasure for us, man. You know we don't have any children of our own," said Lessy.

"Sorry to hear that," said Randy.

"So, you going to be heading up to Curepe?" asked Lessy.

"Well, I figure on travelling until I get a place to rent up there," Randy confirmed.

"And what about the boy?" asked Lessy.

"I have to discuss it with his mother," said Randy.

"You know, it will make us really happy if the boy could stay with us," said Lessy.

"You serious?" Randy asked.

"Yes man, he will be close to the school and we will take good care of him."

"I know that, but I will have to discuss it with his mother," Randy said again.

"You won't have to pay or anything and besides it would be good company for me and the old lady."

"Well the Christmas holidays coming up soon. I will go down and discuss it with she," said Randy.

"If you want, we could go with you too."

"That sound like a good plan to me," said Randy.

Then Vijanti, Naomi and Pedro came outside. Naomi had Ringo in her arms and she brought him over to Lessy. Lessy tickled him under his chin and he started to smile.

"But this fellar turning big man already!"

"Yes, is funny how fast they does grow," said Randy.

"Well, we will have to be going now," said Lessy.

"Take a next one with you padner before you go," Randy urged and Lessy complied.

"To family," he said, and raised his glass.

"To family!" said Randy and Pedro smiled.

The Lessy's home was a simple affair: kitchen, bedroom, a toilet and bath, and an additional bedroom that had been constructed a few months after the abode had been built fifteen years ago. The Lessys used to keep the additional bedroom bright and clean, in expectancy that never materialised. Now they hardly ever went into that room. Dust was everywhere: on the bed, the dressing table and the window sill. Cobwebs hung in the corners and a spider had built its web across the window. After the visit with Randy they began to clean the room.

"You think she will allow him to stay with us?" asked Lessy.

"Well the least that we could do is prepare," said Naomi.

"True," said Lessy, inserting the broom in the spider's web and turning it around, entangling the whole web on the broom – the spider raced up the wall.

"You know, Les, I feel God going to smile on us."

"I hope so, girl."

On the 16th of December, Randy, Lessy and Naomi arrived in Icacos. Louisa Silva knew of their coming from Pedro, who was already home on vacation, and had made elaborate preparations: stewed fish, dumplings, curried shrimp, boiled dasheen and cassava.

Louisa had long forgiven Randy for deserting her and her child. Pedro had come along when Randy was only eighteen and he had cut out and ran away from them, but he had sent money to her whenever he could. As the years rolled by, Louisa realised that he had been too immature at the time to accept responsibilities. Secretly, she had hoped that he would come back to her, but when he got married she knew it was over and that was when she had picked up with Mootilal.

Louisa was the perfect hostess, but Mootilal, very insecure, was hovering around the door like a mean mongrel, watching her every move. She invited him to join them but he refused. After eating, Randy told Louisa about his intentions to move to Curepe and the Lessy's offer. Louisa was silent for a while then she said:

"I will need to think this over. We will be coming to San Fernando next week and I will have an answer for you then."

"Take your time, but you must know that if he stay with us we will treat him like our own son," Lessy said.

They spent the entire day in Icacos and the first chance Louisa got to talk to Randy by himself, she asked him:

"What you personally think of the idea?"

"One thing I know is that they really like Pedro and I personally feel that he would be a lot happier with them, than he is with Vijanti and me," said Randy.

"You should be shame to make a statement like that," said Louisa.

"You asked me for my opinion," Randy shrugged.

"Well at least you honest. Anyways, I would still have to discuss it with Pedro and I will give them an answer sometime next week."

The guests left on the late bus that afternoon, after a truly enjoyable day. Louisa and Pedro sat in their hammock in the gallery speaking, long after their departure. The moon came up over the coconut trees like a huge silver dollar, lending a silvery edge to the darkened silhouette of the trees. Pedro enjoyed the view while his mother questioned him about the Lessys; when she was finished, her mind was made up. She would allow Pedro to stay with them.

Lessy took the knife from Naomi and opened the tin of paint; the paint looked white. He cut a piece of stick about one foot long and began to swirl around the paint in the tin; streaks of blue started to rise to the top. Lessy swirled vigorously with his stick until the paint was completely blue, then he dipped the paint brush, applied it to the wall and stepped back.

"What you think?" he asked.

"Nice colour," Naomi confirmed.

"Think he will like it?"

"Yep, I think he will like It," Naomi smiled.

"But we not even sure if she will allow him to stay," said Lessy.

"You must have faith, Lessy" said Naomi, as he dipped the brush and continued painting.

In quick time, Lessy had one of the walls painted blue and he passed the brush to Naomi who began to try her hand.

"I hearing like somebody calling out in front," the husband said, cocking his ear.

"Yes, you better see who it is," said Naomi and Lessy went to the front of the house.

Randy, Louisa and Pedro were standing outside the Lessy's home.

"Come in, come in," said Lessy.

"We thought nobody was home," said Randy.

"We was in the backroom doing some painting," Lessy smiled, as Naomi came outside and hugged Louisa and Pedro.

"Sit down and let me get something for you all to drink," said Naomi, as Lessy busily began to pull up chairs for the visitors.

Naomi came back with a waiter filled with drinks.

They talked for a while and Louisa said:

"I've made up my mind. I will allow Pedro to stay with you all, but under one condition."

"Okay, and what might that condition be?" asked Lessy.

"That we give you a monthly sum for his upkeep," said Louisa.

"Oh no, please… we can't accept that. We love Pedro like a son," said Naomi.

"But we must give you something to help out," said Randy.

"Please, that will make us feel bad," said Lessy.

"Well?" said Louisa, opening her palms and facing them upward.

Lessy and Naomi broke into bright smiles and Naomi took Louisa by the hand and said:

"Come, let me show you something," and took her into the room that they were painting. "This will be his room. We were just painting when you all came."

"It's very nice," said Louisa.

"We built it hoping that we would have children of our own, now we are so thankful that God has sent someone to occupy it," said Naomi.

"I know that you all will take good care of my son," said Louisa, hugging Naomi.

"You can't believe how happy this will make us," Naomi confessed, tears coming to her eyes.

They went back and joined the others. Lessy, Randy and Pedro were talking about Andy Roberts and Michael Holding, the two, young West Indian fast bowlers who had torn apart the English batting in the test match at old Trafford the day before.

"This might sound like a joke to you, Randy, but I think Pedro has the ability to make it big times as a fast bowler," said Lessy.

"I never see him bowl," said Randy.

"Is all these men does talk 'bout: cricket, cricket, cricket all the time," Naomi, laughed.

"We can't stay too long, because we have to go to High Street to get a couple things for Pedro," said Louisa.

"I was hoping that you all would spend the day," said Naomi.

"Ah next time," Louisa smiled.

When school re-opened in January, Pedro took up residence at the Lessy's. A new pattern began to emerge. He would come home from school, have something to eat, then he would help Lessy for awhile in the garden. After, they would go to the cricket ground, where Lessy taught him the fine art of fast bowling. When they returned home, he would bathe and the three of them would visit Vijanti and little Ringo. They hardly ever met Randy because he came home very late from Curepe. When they got back home, Naomi and Lessy would sit with him and help him with his homework.

In February, Randy got a house to rent in Curepe and Vijanti and Ringo moved in with him. Gradually, Pedro began to improve in his schoolwork and at the end of his first term with the Lessys, he passed all his subjects and his average went up by six percent. The Lessys showered him with all their love and kindness and they taught him discipline and good manners. When Pedro got into form four he was exceptional in cricket. He was a fixture on the San Fernando Secondary Sixteen and Under Cricket Team and was wrecking havoc among the batsmen of the other schools.

Lessy was now spending longer periods with him in the nets at the cricket ground, preparing him for bigger things. He was trying to get him up to maximum speed.

"Your run up to the wicket is a bit too tense, Pedro, you need to relax and run more smoothly. If I could get you to do that you would be unplayable. Tell me something, in what instance do you enjoy running the most?"

Pedro scratched his head, sat down on the grass, playing with the cork ball, and thought for a while. Finally, he smiled, tossed the ball at Lessy, and said:

"When I on the beach and I take a sprint, running hard towards the water to take a dive into the sea… that is when I enjoy running the most."

"Bingo! All you have to do, is when you coming in to bowl, you think that is the sea you going to dive into and that is it!"

Lessy vigorously tossed the ball back to Pedro:

"Now get back to your mark and let's try it."

Lessy picked up the bat and stood in front of the stumps and Pedro came bounding in – smooth, graceful… almost catlike – up to the wicket and bowled. Lessy was so astonished at the speed that the ball almost knocked him down. Over and over he made Pedro bowl and each time he came in faster. Then they sat down on the grass and after some cricket talk, Lessy asked:

"What do you fear most?"

"Fear most?" Pedro scratched his head and instantly said: "*Mr. Screeler.*"

"*Mr. Screeler*?" Lessy asked, bewildered.

"Yes, *Mr. Screeler*. That is the name of the whip that Mr. Ramsook does beat we with in school."

Lessy laughed heartily.

"Okay, then we will call this ball that I am going to teach you, *Mr. Screeler*. You have already mastered the bouncer. *Mr. Screeler* is a ball that you hold across the seam and deliver with the same venom as a bouncer, only, with *Mr. Screeler*, you pitch it a little more up to the batsman. Most of the time the batsman mistakes it for a bouncer and gets into position to hook, only to realise that it is much closer to him and he is unable to make the adjustments. *Mr. Screeler* is the deadliest weapon in a fast-bowler's arsenal... twice as deadly as a bouncer."

Evening after evening, they worked on *Mr. Screeler* until Lessy was satisfied that Pedro had perfected it.

That same year, San Fernando Sec. produced their best ever cricket team in the senior division. The senior team was made up mostly of students from Form Five, Upper Six and Lower Six. This year in question, the seniors made it all the way to the finals in the limited-*overs* competition. The limited-overs competition was a one innings affair, with each side bowling a quota of fifty overs to the other. No bowler was allowed to bowl more than ten overs and the side scoring the most runs was the winner. The other team that reached the final was Couva Secondary. Three days before the final, the senior fast bowler for San Fernando Sec., Gideon Paris, was involved in a car crash and was ruled out of the match. San Fernando Sec. was in a quandary because Gideon was their main strike bowler. A meeting was called, involving the coach, the sports master, the captain and his team, to choose someone to replace Gideon. The coach, who was also the sports master, Mr. Reginald and most of the team were in favour of a fast bowler named Bob

Hope from Upper Six, but Captain Williams had a surprise up his sleeve:

"I have watched the Sixteen and Under Team in their last two matches. There is a young fellow from Form Four, his name is Pedro Silva but they call him Quick Silva. He is very quick, I think even quicker than Gideon. He has my vote to be the replacement."

"That's very irresponsible Captain Williams," Sports Master Reginald said. "We are all familiar with Pedro and know of his great pace, but he is quite young and inexperienced also. Think what a classy batsman like Rupert Callender would do to him. Why, he will tear him to pieces."

"Gideon Paris was our main strike bowler and we have to replace him with someone of genuine pace and Pedro has that quality," Williams countered.

Argument after argument was put forward but in the end the captain had his way and he himself went over to Form Four and told Pedro of his selection. When Pedro reached home that afternoon and gave the news to Lessy he punched the air and yelled "yes!" then he hugged Pedro and said:

"Our hard work has paid dividends sooner than I thought."

The big day had arrived.

It was nine-thirty in the morning, match time, at the Sando Sec. Cricket Ground. The dry season sun was already making its presence felt and the lack of moisture had turned the sky into a brilliant blue; every now and then a tiny, white cloud, like a lost sheep, would make its way across the blue, upper pasture. Already a colourful crowd was scattered around the cricket ground: parents, teachers, past pupils, diehard supporters and cricket lovers, all gathered to lend support to one team or the other.

Lessy, armed with a bell, and Empress Naomi were seated on a bench in front of the woodwork shed. The students of

Sando Sec. huddled together in front of the main school building that stood at the base of the cricket ground.

The two teams lined up on the field to the cheers of the crowd. Dignitaries walked onto the field and shook hands with the players. Then the two captains, accompanied by the two umpires, strode out to the middle for the toss. It was won by Couva Sec. and they elected to bat.

The Couva Sec. opening batsmen began to pad up, while Captain Williams of Sando Sec. began to set his field. There were vendors peddling *snowcones*, sugarcakes and other sweets to noisy spectators; then loud cheering as Henry Roach and Prakash Tewarie, the two opening batsmen made their way to the middle.

Captain Williams handed the ball to his tall, robust *fast bowler*, Rufus Jones. Rufus marked out his run and began to rub the ball vigorously against the right leg of his trousers until it looked like a ripe cherry. The umpire gave the signal to commence play.

Rufus came bounding in, like a raging bull, up to the wicket and delivered, a good ball, on off stump and moving away. Roach came forward tentatively, the ball beating the bat and cannoning into the wicketkeeper's gloves; loud cheers from the Sando Sec. supporters. The next ball was up to Roach and immediately, he got onto the front foot and hammered it back past the bowler, the ball burning the grass on its way to the boundary; loud cheers from the Couva Sec. supporters. A single was taken off the following ball and the rest of the over went by without any addition to the score. Captain Williams went over to Pedro, gave him the ball and said:

"Now youngster, get your line and length correct and then step up the pace."

Pedro's heart was pounding in his chest as he measured out his run.

Lessy began ringing his bell in earnest.

"Come on, son! Come on!" he shouted as Pedro came in off his long run, tall, athletic, gliding up to the wicket, and delivered.

A good length ball of average pace, just outside the off stump and Roach shouldered arms and let it go through to the wicketkeeper. With every ball, Pedro's pace increased and the wicketkeeper had to step back a few paces. There were 'oohs' and 'aahs' coming from the spectators and the Couva Sec. Sports Master leaned over to his Sando Sec. counterpart and whispered:

"Where did you unearth this kid from? We did not see him in the first rounds."

"Just a little surprise, my friend… just a little surprise," replied a just as astounded Mr. Reginald.

They scored one run off the over and Rufus continued at the other end. Roach stroked a four off Rufus's over and in Pedro's next over, things came alive.

First ball: Pedro coming off his long run and a very fast Yorker; Tewarie started to come forward but already the ball was through his defence, uprooting his middle stump and sending it cartwheeling past Wicketkeeper Waldron;

The Sando Sec. supporters were in a frenzy. The students formed a Mexican wave in front the school building and set it in motion by waving their hands simultaneously. The wave was encroaching on the batsmen's side screen so the umpire asked Mr. Reginald to clear the area in front of the screen. Try as he might Mr. Reginald could not get the children to move, so he summoned Mr. Ramsook. The dean strode to the area, *Mr. Screeler* in hand, almost like a gunfighter in a movie and stopped in front the troubled area. Standing about twenty feet in front of the children he used *Mr. Screeler* and drew out the side screen in the air, and then he pointed *Mr. Screeler* to the right. Immediately, the children moved to the right and the side screen was cleared. Cheers went up again and Mr.

Ramsook bowed to the crowd as the new batsman made his way to the middle.

Rupert Callender's reputation had preceded his arrival at Sando Secondary. Callender was the rising star in the Senior Colleges' League and he had already rattled up four centuries in the league and on his debut for the Trinidad Under Nineteen Team had made an enterprising fifty. Callender's ambition as a child was to be a stick fighter. His father Fenton Callender was the most feared stickman in all of Central. A nimble-footed, fearless competitor, Fenton had spilt blood in almost every ring he appeared in. Rupert's mother saw the warrior spirit of her husband in her son but she abhorred violence so she saved up her money and on his tenth birthday, bought him a cricket bat.

"Wield it with the same passion that your father does wield his fighting stick," she said and Rupert did not disappoint her.

Callender sauntered to the wicket. You could almost feel his confidence. A slightly bowlegged walk, he was a natural battle axe. This was the moment the huge crowd was waiting for; they had all come to see Rupert Callender bat. There was cheering all around. Williams came up to Pedro:

"Now youngster, a full head of steam, turn up the tempo and unsettle this peacock."

Pedro came off his long run and delivered a good length ball of electrifying pace just outside the off stump, Callender shouldered arms and allowed the ball to go through to the wicketkeeper; there was a loud thud when the ball entered the gloves. The wicketkeeper whipped out his right glove and shook his hand in the wind, visibly hurt by the pace of the delivery. There was silence all around the ground, but the spectators were moving closer to the playing area. Everyone was sensing the ensuing battle; you could feel it in the air, the young fast bowler versus the master batsman, speed and hostility trying to compromise the calm confidence of the prolific scorer. Pedro got back to his mark and started his run in, up to the wicket, and delivered, very fast but fractionally short outside the off stump. Already, Callender had danced himself into position and with a flick of the wrist, the bat caressed the ball and sent it speeding along the ground through the vacant gully position to the boundary for four. It was a shot of class that sent the crowd into a frenzy. A fellow in the crowd shouted:

"That is the right handed version of Gary Sobers".

"Nah boy, that is the nigger edition of Rohan Kanhai," another fellar shouted.

Everyone laughed.

Williams walked up to Pedro. "Don't let that bother you youngster, you have the pace to undo him."

The batsman settled down again and Pedro came in, right arm, over the wicket, a testing delivery, pitching on middle stump and moving away. Callender came forward tentatively but was beaten for pace, the ball missing the edge of the bat by a whisper and flying through to the wicketkeeper who took it chest height.

"Set him up, Pedro! Set him up!" Ras Lessy chanted, ringing his bell.

Pedro came in with the next ball: it was a bouncer and in a flash Callender was into position and hooking. The ball soared into the air as if it had wings and over the wood work shed for a mighty six; the crowd was enjoying it.

"Introduce him to Mr. Screeler now!" shouted Ras Lessy, ringing his bell passionately.

Pedro took his time going back to his mark, a sly grin playing at the corner of his mouth.

He came bounding in, smooth, catlike, up to the wicket and delivered, just short of a good length and rising. The stick fighter in Callender was already getting into position to hook... and then he started to duck. It came at him like a rocket. Instinctively, the bat handle came up to cover his face. The ball cannoned into his batting gloves and ballooned into the air. Wicketkeeper Waldron stepped back a few paces and took a simple catch. Callender was on his way, removing his batting gloves as he went, blood trickling from the middle finger of his right hand all the way to the pavilion. Ras Lessy ran onto the field and lifted Pedro into the air shouting:

"This is my son! This is my son!"

Satesh, in the excitement, had also found himself on the field. When Ras Lessy put Pedro back on the ground, Satesh folded his fist and gave his partner a *bounce* and ran off the field, straight into the waiting jaws of Mr. Ramsook and *Mr. Screeler*. Mr. Ramsook caught him a good one on his back, but he managed to lose himself between the students, much to the delight of the crowd. With their ace batsman back in the pavilion, panic set into the Couva camp.

The first ball of the next over, bowled by Rufus, is missed by both the batsman and the wicketkeeper and goes all the way to the boundary for four byes. The very next ball, the batsmen attempts an impossible single and Captain Williams, swooping down on the ball, hits the wicket with a direct throw! The new batsman runs out for a duck. The score: twenty four runs for three wickets.

The next batsman, Emanuel Collins, seems intent on taking the bull by its horns; the very first ball he receives, he hits for a mighty six over mid on. The next ball is smacked another lusty blow, over mid wicket this time: another six! The fifth ball, forward defensive and he takes a single off the last ball of the over.

Pedro came bounding in with the first ball of his third over, a real *snorter*, short of a length and rising. Collins, underestimating the pace of the delivery, went into the hook shot, only to top edge the ball unto his right eye brow, opening up a nasty gash that started bleeding profusely. He retired hurt.

The score: thirty-seven runs for three wickets and one man on the way to the hospital.

The next batsman clearly had no stomach for that type of bowling and seemed intent on getting back to the safety of the pavilion as quickly as possible. The first ball he received, he started backing away towards square leg, leaving his three stumps exposed and Pedro's delivery knocked the middle stump out of the ground. Couva Sec. against the ropes and Sando Sec. tightening the screws.

The score: thirty-seven runs for four wickets and one man is arriving at the hospital.

The new batsman, Herelal Capildeo, posted a quick twenty run partnership with Roach before he was caught in the slip in Pedro's fifth over.

The score: fifty-seven runs for five wickets and one man is receiving six stitches over his eyebrow at the hospital.

Captain Williams brings on his spin bowler, Vishal Maraj, to replace Rufus Jones and he bowls a maiden over. Captain Williams walks over to his Vice Captain Waldron:

"The kid is young and he has already bowled five of his allotted overs. Do you think we should give him a rest and bring him back later?"

"The kid is on a roll and he's still bowling very fast. Give him a go at another over and see what happens," replied Waldron.

Captain Williams threw the ball once more to Pedro and he gave it a rigorous rub against his trousers. He could hear Lessy's bell urging him on. Adrenalin pumping… he runs in up to the wicket and delivers, short of a length and rising dangerously; the batsman ducks right into the delivery and is hit flush on the nose. Blood is dripping from his nose unto the matting. He retires hurt and is escorted off the field and into a waiting car. The new batsman takes a single off the first ball and Roach hits Pedro for a boundary off the last ball of the over.

The score: sixty-two runs for five wickets, one man on the way to the hospital with a suspected broken nose and one man coming back from the hospital with six stitches over his right eyebrow.

Vishal Maraj begins a new over and the new batsman takes a cheeky single off the first ball. Second ball: Roach wads into Maraj and hoists him over the woodwork shed; cheers from the Couva spectators. Next ball: Roach is at it again, stepping down the wicket and hitting straight over the bowlers head this time, another mighty six! Couva spectators cheering lustily. The next ball: Vishal gives it a bit more flight and Roach is going again, but this time only manages to hit it high into the air and it falls right into the hands of the man on the long on boundary.

The score: seventy-five runs for six wickets, one man arriving at the hospital with a suspected broken nose and one man arrives back at the cricket ground with six stitches over his eyebrow.

No further runs are scored off Vishals' last, two balls. Captain Williams decides to give Pedro a rest and he calls up his other spin bowler, Andrew Ramkhelawan.

The two batsmen at the crease, Ali and Brown, take the score to ninety-nine and then Ali is bowled by a *Googly* from Ramkhelawan.

The score: ninety-nine for seven, one man at the hospital with a confirmed broken nose and the new batsman coming to the wicket has six stitches over his right eyebrow.

Immediately after Ramkhelawans' over, Williams throws the ball to Pedro.

Ras Lessy now begins to run around in the crowd ringing his bell, his long dreadlocks blowing in the wind like a lion's mane.

"Finish them off, Pedro!" he shouted.

The batsman takes a single off his first delivery and brings up the hundred. Loud cheers from the Couva supporters.

The man with the six stitches comes down to face the bowling. Pedro turns and comes steaming in and delivers a very fast *Yorker* – the man with the stitches is afraid to play forward and starts to back away and his middle stump is uprooted.

The score: one hundred for eight as the man with the six stitches walks contentedly back to the pavilion. The new batsman tickles one on the leg side and starts off immediately for the run; his partner wants no part of that single and sends him back; the throw hits the wicket before he arrives and it's all over.

The score: one hundred for nine and one man officially warded at the San Fernando General Hospital with a broken nose.

Sando Sec. started badly, losing their first two wickets for only ten runs. Then Captain Williams came to the crease and steadied the ship. He remained to the very end, scoring a brilliant fifty-three, as Sando Sec. cruised to one hundred and one for the loss of five wickets.

Sando Sec. had won their first Islandwide Trophy and Pedro Silva was the man of the moment. The two teams lined up for the presentation. First, silver medals were presented to all the Couva Secondary School players; then, gold medals to all the Sando Secondary School players. Then the adjudicator came forward to select the man of the match. He took the microphone, looked at the crowd, relished the suspended animation and announced:

"I want to make mention of Mr. Roach of Couva Secondary who stayed around for a while in the face of some very hostile bowling. Also I must mention Captain Williams of Sando Secondary for his match-winning innings of fifty-three runs. But, the man of the match goes to… Pedro Silva! For capturing five wickets in a devastating display of fast bowling!"

Pedro went forward and collected his Man of the Match trophy, to great applause, then he walked over to the crowd and gave the trophy to the Empress and the medal to Lessy.

"I want you all to have these," said Pedro.

"But you won them, we want you to keep them," Lessy whispered.

"No. I want you to have them," said Pedro and he placed his arms around his parents.

Pedro went on to obtain all his passes and won a sports scholarship to study in England. When he was finished, he became a professional cricketer and when his team was playing in a final at Lords, he sent tickets for Lessy and Naomi to come to England.

They had a wonderful time.

Later on, he married a beautiful girl of Jamaican and English parentage, the kind they refer to as a *red dougla*. He bought a car in England and shipped it down to the Lessy's as a present. He sent regular sums to Randy and his family and Louisa and Mootilal. Then he brought his wife to Trinidad to meet his family and on the third day, when Lessy and the Empress were taking him and his wife for a drive up High Street, he noticed a short fellow, with his hair sticking out of his head like pickers, holding hands with a beautiful Indian girl.

"Stop! Please stop!" said Pedro and as Lessy brought the car to a halt he opened the door, ran across the street, bolted up the pavement and touched the fellow on his shoulder.

"Satesh!"

"Pedro! Whey the hell is this, boy! You get tall like a coconut tree!"

They embraced and Satesh introduced Pedro to his wife, Basanti.

"I have heard so much about you," said Pedro, then he took them across to meet his family.

After Satesh was introduced to Pedro's wife, he pulled him aside and whispered in his ears:

"You lucky I done marry my Basanti, else I take away this nice *red dougla* woman from you right now."

Pedro laughed and playfully rang one of Satesh ears with his right hand. He joked:

"Boy, behave yourself, before I go and borrow *Mr. Screeler* from Ramsook and let you have a couple on your back."

The Bull

Hubert held fast to the rope as the bull kept pulling him away from the pen.

"Bentley! Come and give me a hand quick with the bull before it break loose, boy," he said.

Bentley was sitting on the banister, his back arched against the wall.

"Sell the blasted animal if you can't handle it," he muttered under his breath and made no attempt to move.

"Claris! Tell you blasted, lazy, good-for-nothing son to give me a hand with the bull!" Hubert shouted to his wife.

Claris walked out into the gallery and placed her hands on her waist.

"Why the hell you buy bull for? Ent you is cowboy? Handle it for yuhself!" she said.

By now the bull had broken free from Hubert and was racing towards the neighbour's garden. He let out a string of expletives as he chased after it. Bentley steupsed and maintained his position. Claris disparaged:

"Don't worry with your father, boy, he playing cowboy in his old days. He could ah give me the money he pay for that bull to buy a stove. Instead, he have me cooking on a fireside like a prehistoric woman. Let him haul his arse and run after he bull for he self."

Hubert managed to restrain the bull and came tugging it back, step-by-step, bull and man in a tug of war. Finally, he got it into the pen. He bolted the door, looked up at the sky and raised his hands into the air and shouted:

"Why the hell I didn't plant cassava instead of laying with Claris and creating that wicked, lazy, son-of-a-bitch Bentley?"

Bentley steupsed, got off the banister and went inside the house. Hubert came up the steps and entered behind him.

"Claris, I trying my best to make a man out of that boy, but you keep pampering him like a five year old. Bentley is nineteen years old and is high time he start helping around the place. Now make haste and put some breakfast on the table for me," he said.

"Listen mister-man, yuh feel I didn't hear you out there, saying how you regret you lay with me? Well from now on, you will rely on that blasted bull in the pen to make breakfast for you. Now haul you arse out of my way and let me pass!"

"Ah man can't even say something in his own house now," said Hubert sadly, shaking his head.

He walked over to the hat rack, still shaking his head, plucked off his Wilson, donned it and ambled through the doorway. Down the steps and across to the bull pen he went.

"Here boy, here boy," he said gently. The bull nosed up to him and Hubert began to scratch his head. "All this damn commotion is because I buy you," he said to the bull.

The bull, seeming to understand, shook its head up and down against his fingers and Hubert began to scratch a little harder.

"All she studying is stove and fridge, she don't understand the principles of commerce."

The bull bellowed in agreement and Hubert continued:

"Ent when I finish build my cart you would pull it and we will get odd jobs around the village and we would take the money from them jobs and buy stove and fridge for she?"

The bull moved its head up and down again.

"A bull could work and buy stove and fridge, but you ever see a stove or fridge working to buy a bull. Stupid woman.

Simple thing like that, she can't understand. She and that lazy son of hers," said Hubert, patting the bull on its head.

He began walking towards the road. He turned right and strolled the quarter of a miles distance to his younger brother's home. Sam was sitting on his step sipping his morning coffee when Hubert strode in.

"Morning, Sam."

"Morning, big brother."

"How Myra?"

"She's okay. Coffee?"

"Yes please."

"Myra, bring some coffee for Hubert please," said Sam.

Myra looked through the kitchen window.

"Morning Hube. How Claris?"

"Morning sis, Claris good and youself?"

"Good, good," said Myra as she disappeared into the kitchen.

Sam swirled the coffee around in his cup and took a little sip.

"So how is my nephew Bentley?" he asked.

"Lazy as ever, ah just can't seem to get the fellar going," said Hubert.

Sam chuckled. "There must be something that he like."

"Fete and girls of course. The only time he gets off that banister is when a girl pass on the road. Immediately, he does change from a hibernating bear to a strutting peacock."

"It have a programme where they does send young fellars to do agriculture work in Canada, why you don't carry him to sign up?"

"Once is work, I will have to tie him up to get him there," Hubert replied.

Myra came with the coffee and placed a plate filled with saltfish accras on the step between the two brothers.

"Thanks, Myra" said Hubert, holding the coffee in one hand as the other reached into the plate and lifted out an accra.

"So how the bull?" asked Sam.

"Boy, that bull is a real bone of contention between Claris and me, but he coming along nice."

Sam laughed.

"But you should still tell Bentley 'bout this Canada thing."

"Hear what, you and he does get along good. Why you don't pass by this afternoon and have a talk with him? He does listen to you," Hubert said, lifting off another accra from the plate.

"Okay, I will pass by this evening. How Claris?"

"Claris good, is just that she spoiling the boy beyond repairs," said Hubert as he got up and drained the last, few drops of coffee into his mouth. "Myra! Thanks for the coffee! Ah leaving!" he shouted and then he turned to Sam: "Ah seeing you later?"

"Yes, ah will come."

Hubert was nearing the house. He could see Bentley holding down his usual position on the bannister. When Bentley saw him coming, he joined his thumb and index finger on his right hand into a circle, closed one eye and looked at his father through it, then he brought the circle closer to his eye, like a telescope, and he turned Hubert into an old cowboy riding a brown and white horse. Slowly they came, the old cowboy and his horse. Wait! They are headed towards the bull pen; the bull pen vanishes and the bull is standing on the grass of the prairies. The old cowboy is circling with his horse, rope in hand; he sends out his lasso and encircles the neck of the bull. The bull does not like the feel of rope against his neck and he heads off in the opposite direction, but wait! The old cowboy forgets to tie the rope to his saddle and the bull yanks the rope and sends him flying into the air and he lands flat on his back, in a big load of shit, which the bull himself had deposited there a few minutes before. He gets up now, he's covered in bull shit, he's headed towards the house, he's climbing the steps, he's in the gallery–

"Why the arse you looking at me through that circle in your finger for?" Hubert demanded.

Bentley dropped his hand to his lap and smiled mischievously. Hubert went into the house, stood in front of the hat rack, took the Wilson off his head and began spinning it around in his hand, then he placed it on the rack. He walked towards the kitchen. Through the half-opened bedroom door he could see the dirty soles of Claris feet as she lay on the bed. Into the kitchen and he could see that Claris had left his breakfast on the table. He smiled to himself. *Good ole girl,* he thought. She was only threatening him, but he would play her the same game, he would not touch it. His belly was filled with Myra's accra anyway. Down the back step he went. He picked up his hoe, opened the back gate and went into his garden. He started to check the tomato trees that he had transplanted two weeks before: twenty-one standing and three down. He knelt before one of the fallen trees and tried propping it up by placing soil around the roots. The plant collapsed again.

"Blasted mole crickets," he muttered.

He got up, picked up the hoe and gently began moulding the standing trees. The sun was climbing in the sky. Beads of perspiration began forming above his brow and Hubert flicked them away with his index finger.

He heard a sound and looked over at the mango tree. A ripe mango had fallen off the tree and was rolling down an incline. Hubert saw it, dropped the hoe and went after it. He picked up the mango, swiped away the milk, which was trickling from the stem, on his trousers and sat down on the ground, with his back against the trunk of the mango tree. Hubert took the mango and began polishing it against his trousers, and then he held it to his mouth. First, he bit into the skin and pushed the mango upwards, peeling off a piece of the skin, then he spun the mango around and repeated the process until he had all the skin off. He then began to eat the flesh. The juice trickled down his hands, all the way to his elbows, and when all the flesh was gone, he began sucking the seed and nibbling at it with his teeth. The seed turned from yellow to a *creamish*-white. He held the seed in his hand. A fowl was scratching around in the garden. Hubert closed one of his eyes and took aim. He flung the seed at the fowl, hitting it on its feet. The fowl made a desperate cackle, flew into the air and landed a few feet away and hustled off on its legs. Hubert smiled. He used his shirt sleeve to wipe the mango juice from around his mouth, then he pushed himself forward until he was lying on the ground, crossed his two hands over his chest and fell asleep.

Sam pulled on his trousers, buckled his belt and then he strapped on his sandals.

"You will tell Claris hello for me," said Myra.

"Okay," said Sam as he strode through the door and walked out to the road. Sam always looked forward to his chats with Bentley whom he found to be rather amusing. Bentley was a carbon copy of a younger Hubert and Hubert was seeing his own youthful, dreamy, lazy self mirrored in Bentley and that, Sam thought, was the source of their problems. He walked leisurely along the road, calling out to neighbours as he went. He could see his brother's house in the distance and already he could see the familiar figure of Bentley sitting on the banister. When he reached in front of the house, Bentley called out to him:

"Aye, Uncle Sam, what happening dey, boy?"

"Good, good Bentley and yourself?" Sam replied, entering the yard.

"I good man," said Bentley, jumping off the bannister and running down the steps to greet his uncle.

They shook hands and Uncle Sam asked:

"Tell me, Bentley, how come you always sitting on that banister when I pass around?"

"Oh, I just like to catch breeze and look at the road," said Bentley.

"Look at the road, or look at the girls when they passing on the road?" asked Sam.

Bentley laughed, *che-he-he*, while Uncle Sam, who was now under the house, opened the hammock and slipped into it.

"How you know is girls ah does be looking at, Uncle Sam?" asked Bentley.

"You forget I was young too," said Sam.

"You look like you was a real rooster in your days," said Bentley.

Sam smiled.

"How come my father does not talk to me like this?" continued Bentley.

"Well boy, father responsibility and uncle responsibility is two different thing, you know," said Sam.

Bentley puckered his lips. "I see what you mean," he said.

"Where you father?" asked Sam.

"He gone in the garden."

"And you mother?"

"She taking a rest," said Bentley.

"Well, it doh matter, because is really you I come to talk to. It have a programme where they sending young fellars to work in Canada," said Sam.

"What kind of work?" asked Bentley.

"Farm work," said Sam.

"That is real hard work, boy!" said Bentley, his eyes losing interest.

"Yes, but they paying good, and besides, I hear it does have a lot of extra-curricular activities up there," enticed Sam.

"Like what?" asked Bentley.

"Like girls, Bentley… girls by the bag loads."

Bentley's eyes brightened.

"They does have party up there?" he asked.

"Boy, Canada is the party capital of the world, every weekend is a party up there," said Sam.

Bentley eyes were now gleaming.

"How you does sign up?" asked Bentley.

"You have to go to the ministry in San Fernando and apply. You have you passport?" asked Sam.

"Yes," replied Bentley.

"Well, you halfway there and you rel lucky because next week Monday I going to San Fernando," Sam cajoled.

"I could go with you?" asked Bentley.

"Of course," said Sam.

Monday morning, Bentley dressed up sharp, sharp and armed with a brown, paper bag containing birth certificate, school-leaving certificate and passport, he and Uncle Sam, board a taxi and headed for San Fernando. When he get there, they made him full out a couple of forms and sent him for a medical checkup.

In a few weeks time, Bentley on board one of them big airplanes headed for Canada. When the plane landed, they walk through something like a tube and ended up in the immigration department. The liaison officer, a Trinidadian fellow with a heavy Canadian accent, came and took out all the farm workers from the line. He huddled them into a corner, took their passports and proceeded to have them cleared. When he came back, he gave them their passports. Then he separated them into groups of five, four, three, two and even one man was left standing over by himself. Bentley was in the group of two with an Indian fellow. Then a white fellow came and the liaison officer pointed to the group of four standing in the corner.

"There is your guys," he said and the white man went over, shook hands with them and they went away together.

A little while after, along comes a short, white guy, walking with a limp and the liaison officer pointed over to Bentley and the Indian.

"Is that my stock?" he asked, as if he was talking about cattle. He went over to Bentley and the Indian. "Hey *Lalbarry*, I see you have made it back," he said, addressing the Indian and shaking his hand.

"Is Lalbeharry, Boss," corrected the Indian.

"Whatever!" said the white man, then he turned to Bentley and looked at him from head to toe. "Can you do farm work?" he asked.

Bentley puff up his chest like a strong man. "You asking a duck if he could swim!"

"We'll see, we'll see," said the farmer, as he turned and limped out of the airport with Lalbeharry and Bentley following him.

When Bentley came out of the airport, he was hit, for the first time, by the coldness that the month of March bestows on visitors to Canadian soil. Bentley, who was not properly dressed for the occasion, start to tremble like a leaf. His teeth start to knock like the tappets in an automobile engine and Bentley swore that he was going to freeze to death. He stuck his hands in his pockets and started a kind of jog-walk. Two beautiful girls, who were coming from the opposite direction, looked at Bentley's amusing antics and began to laugh, but Bentley, feeling so cold he didn't even notice the chicks. They had reached the farmers truck and the farmer looked at Bentley, shivering from head to toe, shook his head and said:

"Looks like you're in for a hard trip this time, *Lalbarry*."

"Is Lalbeharry, Boss. Lal-be-harry."

"Funny sort of name if you ask me," he said.

The farmer started his truck and began to drive away from the city. Bentley started to relax, enjoying the warmth in the vehicle. Leaving the city behind, they entered the suburbs and then they headed to forested area. On and on they drove and Bentley start to get uneasy. All he seeing was coniferous forest on both sides of the road. Then they left the main highway and turned right onto a secondary road and in the middle of nowhere they came upon the farm. It stood on a huge clearing in the middle of the forest.

Lalbeharry came out of the truck and opened the gate and the farmer drove up to the bunk house. The farmer came out of the truck, took a key out of his pocket and opened the bunk house door, then he turned to Bentley:

"Welcome to hell, boy. What did you say your name was?"

"Bentley," he said, trembling like a leaf.

"Well, Bentley, I am Van Swam. Work begins at six tomorrow morning and ends at four in the evening. We work from Sunday to Sunday, but on Sundays we let you off at twelve o'clock so that you can do your laundry and prepare your meals for the rest of the week. I'll pass by every morning at five o'clock to wake you all, so that you will have one hour to organise yourself before reporting for duty." Then he turned to Lalbeharry, "Everything is just as you had left it. See that Bentley settles in and then you all can come up to the house and collect your gear," he said and left.

"Boy... I freezing to death," said Bentley, his teeth chattering with coldness. Lalbeharry rushed over to the heater and turned it on. Gradually the heat began to circulate through the musty bunkhouse. Bentley start to cuss:

"What the hell I really get myself into. I can't take this blasted coldness and this white man drive for four hours and wait until he reach here to introduce hisself. On top of that, he watching we like if we is some sort of animals or something that he own."

"Take it easy, padner," said Lalbeharry, lighting the stove and putting on a pot with water to boil.

"How the hell they expect we to work in this kind of coldness?" asked Bentley.

"You will get accustom," said Lalbeharry, adding some coffee to the boiling water and stirring it with a spoon. Then he poured in some milk and sugar and stirred it again. He turned off the stove, took a piece of cloth, held on to the hot pot and poured coffee into two cups. He passed a cup to Bentley. Bentley blew off the smoke and took a sip. The heat from the coffee transferred to Bentley's body and he felt better.

"What! You could make good coffee, boy!" he said.

"Yes man, I is Lalbeharry, from Princess Town," he said, holding out his hand to Bentley, who shook it.

"I's Bentley from Cedros."

"Wait, I know couple people from on your side, man."

"Don't make joke," said Bentley.

"Yes man, you know the Rampauls and the Marcelles? And wait… yes man, the fellar that own the big dance hall… Mr. Curry?" asked Lalbeharry.

"Buh wait, is a small world, man, all these people is my neighbours," said Bentley.

Lalbeharry took the piece of cloth, held the hot coffee pot and refilled his cup.

"You want some more?" he asked.

"Yeh please," said Bentley.

Lalbeharry replenished his cup. "We have to go up by the farmer's house in a while, so is best we tidy up the place," said Lalbeharry, placing his empty cup in the sink and taking up a broom.

He began to sweep the Bunk house. Bentley washed the coffee pot and the two dirty cups, then he began to make up the beds. After, Bentley put on an extra suit of clothes and they took the stroll to the farmer's house. It was just about one hundred yards but outside was beastly cold. Bentley placed his hands in his pockets, his two knees knocking together as he walked. When they got to the farmer's house, he took them to a store room and gave them, boots, gloves and coats to fit. The farmer eyeing Bentley suspiciously, the way how he trembling, and wondering in his old, commercial mind if this young fellow would be able to work in the cold climate. Both men went back to the bunkhouse and retired to their beds. Lalbeharry was quickly off to sleep but Bentley lay there, wide awake, already homesick and thinking about Hubert and Claris. Suddenly he realised how much they meant to him, then slowly he drifted off to sleep.

"Wakey! Wakey! Rise and shine!" shouted Van Swam and he began pounding on the door.

"Okay… okay," answered Lalbeharry.

"Time to get up and boil your coffee boys!" said Van Swam.

Lalbeharry got up and shook Bentley. Bentley sat up yawning.

"What it is I really get myself into?" mused Bentley.

"We have one hour, take you time an put on your full kit, outside will be biting cold. I go cook up something fast," said Lalbeharry.

By the time Bentley done dress, Lalbeharry have food smoking on the table. They eat, sit a while and Van Swam came blowing outside.

"Brace yourself," said Lalbeharry, as he opened the door and when the door opened, is like the north pole make a big yawn into the bunk house.

Bentley start to shiver like a leaf. He bolt inside the van and close the door quickly. Van Swam drove around to the back of his house where he had a whole pile of lumber.

"Okay *Lalkeharry*, you know the set up, I want you to build four, small, green houses for me, five by five metres each," Van Swam ordered.

Lalbeharry and Bentley get to work, but they making slow progress in the cold. Lalbeharry use an electric saw to cut up the lumber into sizes but when is time to nail, trouble start.

Bentley trembling so bad that he can't hold the nail in his hand to nail the wood together. When he bend down, he can't straighten up and when he straighten up, he getting trouble to bend down. Luckily, Lalbeharry was an old hand and he had a lot of patience. By the end of the day, they complete one-and-a-half green house. The farmer start to curse, but Bentley feeling so cold he can't summon the fire to curse back the farmer. Is Lalbeharry that say:

"Take it easy, Boss. You have to give we a little chance to acclimatise."

The next day, the boys doing a little better. Bentley take off his gloves and holding the hammer with his bare hands and nailing with good speed. When lunchtime reach and they ready to eat, big trouble, the place so cold the hammer stick to Bentley's hand and he can't let go of it. Lalbeharry have to warm water in a pot and put Bentley hand and the hammer into the pot of water. When the hammer come off, piece of Bentley skin come off with it too. Bentley started to cry for his mother. It took them three days to finish the green houses.

On the fourth day, Van Swam took them over to his big, green house where he already had all his tomatoes, sweet peppers and onion seedlings planted. Their job was to pull out the weeds from between the seedlings, so the boys down on their knees pulling weeds all day. At the end of the day, they real tired so they gone to bed early.

Four o'clock in the morning, the coldness waked Bentley up. Bentley can't move, his body like a solid block of ice, he ain't even shivering. He tried to call out to Lal but he can't open his mouth. Bentley know what he have to do. He right on the edge of the bed so he just rolled and dropped himself. Bentley crashed to the floor, making a noise like a block of ice cracking into pieces. He moved his toes; they moved. Then he tried his fingers; they moved. He raised his upper body into a sitting position and began to tremble violently.

"Lal… Lal," he called softly.

"What happen Bentley?" asked Lalbeharry, he too shivering.

"Something wrong, boy, it making too cold."

"Oh shit! Like the gas done, boy. The heater not working," trembled Lalbeharry.

He got up, put on the lights and went into the kitchen area. He searched around until he found the little portable electric heater, took it back to the bedroom and plugged it in. Both men put on extra clothes and huddled around the little heater. Bentley began to cry.

"Lal, I going back home boy, I can't take it no longer."

"Take it easy, Bentley. What you going to do when you get back home?" asked Lalbeharry.

"I don't know," said Bentley.

"Listen man, you must have a plan. This is the third year I coming up here. You think I did have to come back? No, but I have a plan. Fellars making real money hauling gravel in Trinidad, so I decide I want to buy one of them big dump trucks. I save up my money from the last two years, but I still couldn't reach the price. I doh believe in taking loans, so I come back, when I finish this hitch, I go have enough money to buy my truck. As soon as I reach Trinidad, I going straight by Charles Mc Earnest. I paying them cash money and driving out of there in one of them nice, new, shiny truck. Is all about sacrifice, Bentley. So what is you plan?"

"My plan is to catch the first plane going back to Trinidad," shivered Bentley.

"Listen man, from what you tell me your old lady and old man catching hell in Trinidad. Right?" asked Lalbeharry.

"Right," agreed Bentley.

"Well, you getting a chance here to do something for them. The work hard, yes, and the conditions rough, but the money good. What your old man does do for a living?" asked Lalbeharry.

"He does plant crops and sell," said Bentley.

"Well if you don't have a plan, join in with the old man. You in the right place here to learn about crops. Why you don't stay and make out your six months? While you here, try to learn up all the new techniques these white people develop in planting vegetables. Before you leave ask Van Swam to take you to one of them agro shops and you buying up portions of all them high bred seeds that they have: tomatoes, sweet peppers, cucumbers and some chemicals too. When you get back to Trinidad, you and the old man team up and get into business. The next thing you know, I might have to come with my dump truck to transport tomatoes and sweet peppers to the market for allyuh," coaxed Lalbeharry.

Bentley's face brightened.

"You know, what you saying make sense," said Bentley.

"Of course. Listen, sacrifice and make out the six months, you will make enough money for you and the old man to go into business and next year you don't have to come back here and put up with Van Swam and his bullshit," said Lalbeharry.

Bentley got up and started pacing the floor.

"You know Lal, you give me a good idea, I going to stay and make my time," said Bentley.

"Wakey! Wakey! Rise and shine, boys!" came Van Swam's voice and he began knocking on the door.

"Wakey, wakey my arse! You didn't know the gas was low, yuh cheap bitch? It done last night and me and Lal nearly freeze to death!" shouted Bentley.

"Oh hell, one of you come with me quickly, let us go up to the house and get another cylinder," said Van Swam.

The month of April came and the place was still very cold. The farmer started to transplant his seedlings from the greenhouse into the fields and Bentley and Lalbeharry were faced with their sternest test: the farmer, sitting inside the planter machine and driving in comfort with his heater on while Bentley and Lal in the open back, with the cold wind piercing their bones, shredding out onion seedlings with their bare hands. The seedlings fine like thread so they can't use gloves. The coldness cracking their hands and blood mingling with the seedlings making it difficult to sow them. Tears rolling down Bentley's cheeks but he not giving up, because, at last he have a plan.

In the month of May the farmer, in a hurry to get in his crops, offered the boys overtime work; he paying in cash. Bentley looked at Lalbeharry.

"What you think?" he asked.

"Well is money we looking for, I say let we take it. You could use the extra cash to buy up your high bred seeds and chemicals to take back to Trinidad," said Lalbeharry.

So the boys start to put in some heavy overtime. In the night, when they come in from work, they could hardly keep their eyes open but they sit down there with pen and paper, checking hours and money like if they working in bank. One night, just after twelve, the weather station predicted heavy frost and Van Swam got up and hurried over to the bunk house. He beat on the door and demanded:

"Wakey! Wakey! Rise and shine, niggers!"

They awoke and checked the clock. Lalbeharry and Bentley start to cuss:

"Is only ten-past-twelve, honky, take a blasted hike!"

Van Swam snarled:

"Get your black asses up! We have to turn on the sprinklers to save the plants from the frost."

It have so much coldness in he voice that Lalbeharry and Bentley rush out without any set of clothes and ran between the rows of plants, turning on the sprinklers. Van Swam was almost impressed and invited them to the farmhouse for coffee. Lalbeharry and Bentley so vex they blank Van Swam's sudden offer.

"Keep your damn coffee!"

The next week, on a sunny day, when Bentley and Lalbeharry were pulling weeds from between the plants, Lalbeharry suddenly yelled:

"Run, boy! Run!"

He himself covered his head and ran towards the bunk house as hail, as large as stones, rained down from the sky. Bentley, bewildered, looked up and didn't know if to run or stand up because is like the whole of Canada was pelting him with stones. When the first one hit him, he run.

Time fly quickly and one week before their departure, Bentley get Van Swam to take him to an agro shop where he made a heavy investment in seeds and chemicals. Then he asked Van Swam to take him to a store where he bought some presents for those back home. The day of their departure, Van Swam took them to the airport and when they got there he turned to Lalbeharry:

"Well Lalbeharry, guess I'll be seeing you next year," he said.

"Jeez, Boss, you finally get it right man and you pronounce it like a real Indian too. Lal-be-harry… about next year, I not too sure," he laughed.

Van Swam turned to Bentley. "Well Bentley, to tell the truth, I was pretty worried about you in the beginning but you turned out to be worth your weight in gold. Will I be seeing you next year?" he asked.

"Time will tell," said Bentley.

They shook hands and left him behind.

Bentley and Lalbeharry so tired that they sleep through the entire flight to Trinidad. Lalbeharry brother came to the airport with a car to pick him up and Bentley get a lift with them to San Fernando. Bentley and Lalbeharry promise to meet again and Bentley with his two, big bags, hire a taxi to take him to Cedros. When Bentley get home, he just put down his two bags, kiss his mother and asked:

"Where Father?"

"You father gone by yuh Uncle Sam," said Claris.

Bentley ain't say another word. He just dive in his bed and was off to sleep immediately. The next day Bentley get up about ten o'clock. When he opened his eyes Claris was standing at his bedside looking at him.

"I thought you would a never wake up, boy," she said.

"Girl, I tired for days. Where Father?" he asked.

"You father gone in the garden," said Claris.

Bentley took a good stretch and got off the bed. Claris had his breakfast on the table. He brushed his teeth and ate. Then he went out into the gallery and looked over at the bull pen.

"Where the bull?" asked Bentley.

"Your father sell it to buy ah stove for me," said Claris.

Bentley ain't say another word, put on a good suit of clothes, take a wad of money, catch a taxi and went to Cap-de-ville. He dropped off by a fellar name Procop, who was his father's good friend. Procop was a butcher; he bought bulls, fattened them and slaughtered them.

"Ay Bentley, I didn't know you come back, boy. How the old man?" asked Procop.

"I ain't see him since I come," said Bentley.

"So what brings you up here?" asked Procop.

"I want to buy a bull," said Bentley.

"But allyuh is real funny people, yes. Just last month yuh father sell me a bull, now you come to buy bull."

"But why allyuh Cap-de-ville people like to mind people business so?" laughed Bentley.

Procop lead Bentley to the back of the house, where he had a stall with about eight bulls.

"What you want to do with this bull?" asked Procop.

"I want him to pull a plough," said Bentley.

"Well you see that brown fellar with the white spot on his head, that is the real man for you. He use to pull cart before," said Procop.

"How much for him?" asked Bentley.

"Twelve hundred and fifty dollars," said Procop.

"And how much to transport him back to Cedros?" asked Bentley.

"One hundred dollars," said Procop.

"One hundred!" But how allyuh butcher people know big money so?" exclaimed Bentley.

"You just like your blasted father! Just pay the twelve-fifty and I will transport it for free," laughed Procop.

When they got to Cedros, Procop reversed his truck to the open pen and they put the bull in. Claris came out into the gallery. Procop said:

"Claris, whey that good-for-nothing man of yours?"

"He still in the garden, buh whey allyuh get that bull from?" asked Claris.

"Bentley buy it for he father," said Procop.

Claris steupsed and went back inside. Bentley and Procop went under the house and Procop sat in the hammock. Bentley took the wad of money out of his pocket and counted out twelve hundred and fifty dollars and passed it to Procop. Procop took a receipt book and pen out of his pocket, placed the carbon paper in the right place and made out a receipt. He tore out the original copy and passed it to Bentley.

"I was hoping to see you father, but it getting late, you will tell him hello for me," said Procop, rising up from the hammock and walking towards his truck.

"I will do that, and thanks for everything," said Bentley.

"Claris! I gone, girl!" shouted Procop.

Claris did not answer.

Bentley took a cutlass, went to the side of the road, cut some grass and gave it to the bull. Then he drew a bucket of water from the well and gave it to the animal. He was about to go up the steps, when he saw Hubert coming through the back gate. Bentley hid behind one of the house pillars and waited for Hubert to pass him. Without warning, he came out and grabbed Hubert behind his neck. Hubert was startled.

"But what the…"

Bentley let go of him and started to laugh.

"Bentley, you son-of-a-bitch! You wouldn't change at all eh, boy!" But Hubert was grinning from ear-to-ear. He hugged Bentley then held him at arm length. "But a-a! Look how you turn big man in six, short months, nah!" Hubert exclaimed.

Bentley laughed.

"I thought the bull must be kill you by now," joked Bentley.

"Nah boy, you mother was missing you too bad, so I sell the bull and buy stove for she, to cheer she up," said Hubert.

"But I could ah swear that I just see the bull in the pen," said Bentley.

"Nah, he gone since last month," replied Hubert.

"Nah, I sure I see a bull in the pen. Come let we go and see," said Bentley.

As they came out into the open, Hubert saw the massive, brown bull with the white spot on its forehead. Hubert whistled low.

"Whey that giant come from, boy?" he asked.

"You son buy it for you," shouted Claris, who had returned to the gallery.

Hubert patted the bull on his head.

"This is what I call bull!" he said to Bentley.

They went into the house where Claris had their food on the table. They sat down and ate heartily. Then Bentley opened one of the bags and gave them the presents he brought for them. After, Bentley and Hubert went into the gallery and as Bentley was about to sit down on the banister, Hubert said:

"I was hoping that you would give that spot a rest when you come back."

Bentley laughed and sat down on a chair instead.

"So how Uncle Sam and Aunt Myra?" asked Bentley.

"They good. You want to take a walk and check them?"

"Nah, it done late already. I will check them tomorrow and besides I wanted to talk with you."

Bentley got off the chair, went inside and came back with the bag filled with seeds and chemicals. He placed it before Hubert and opened it.

"Whey you get all this garden stuff from?" inquired Hubert.

"I buy it for we to go into business," said Bentley.

"But we will have to clean the whole three acres to plant all this," said Hubert.

"That is the idea, Father. You plant big, you reap big," said Bentley.

"But that will take some doing, boy," cautioned Hubert.

"How much land you have clear right now?" asked Bentley.

"About half-acre."

"That is a good start. Tomorrow, I going by the fabricator fellow in Point Fortin and explain to him a type of plough I want him to build for the bull to pull. Then we going to build the boxes for the seedlings, fill them up with manure and plant the seeds. While the seedlings growing, we preparing the land, no slash and burn though that is bad practice, and by the time we get the plough is just to hook it up to the bull and plough the land. By the time we finish, the seedlings in prime to transplant."

"That is a boss plan! When you go Point Fortin tomorrow, I going to start to make the boxes. I have some old board and nails there," said Hubert.

"Right man, and from there, is just: Forward ever! Backward never!"

In no time at all, they have the seeds planted and they begin to clear the land until they bring it clean like a whistle. By this time, they get the plough and while the seedlings growing Bentley and Hubert hook up the bull and start to plough the land into neat rows. They ploughed until the sun was high up in the sky. Bentley said:

"Father, I need to take a lil res."

"You go along boy, the old man could handle hisself," said Hubert.

Bentley walked to the edge of the land and sat down under the shade of a calabash tree. He joined his thumb and index finger into a circle, closed his left eye and brought the circle close to his right eye. He turned his father into Van Swam and he turned the bull into the Dutchman's big combine harvester. The field became covered with ripe tomatoes. He could see Lalbeharry driving up with his big dump truck. Then he could see himself, Hubert and Lalbeharry loading the dump truck with tomatoes for the market. Bentley relaxed his fingers and started to laugh. He looked back at the field and he could see Hubert struggling in the heat to move the bull along. He got to his feet and went back to him.

"Go and take a rest, father, and watch how young boy does work bull."

Hubert trudged over to the calabash tree and sat down. He looked at Bentley, tall and strong, leading the bull at a brisk pace and marvelled at the change that had come over his boy.